RUN FROM THE NUN!

RUN
FROM THE
NUN!

by Erin MacLellan

HOLIDAY HOUSE / New York

1   3   5   7   9   10   8   6   4   2

Library of Congress Cataloging-in-Publication Data

MacLellan, Erin.
    Run from the nun! / by Erin MacLellan.—1st ed.
        p. cm.
    Summary: Hoping to escape from St. Joan of Arc School and
return to her former elementary school, fifth-grader Kara is joined by
some new classmates as she devises schemes to get expelled and as
they all investigate the suspicious actions of the school janitor.
    ISBN 0-8234-1796-4
    [1. Catholic schools—Fiction.   2. Schools—Fiction.
3. Friendship—Fiction.   4. Humorous stories.]   I. Title.

PZ7.M22465Ru 2003
[Fic]—dc21   2003047850

To my parents, Joanne and the late Jack MacLellan,
who nurtured me, read my earliest stories,
and passed on their love of writing and reading.

With love and gratitude to my husband,
Greg Myers, who always believed in me, and
to my son, Jake, who brings me joy and humor each day.

To my critique group friends
who helped me along the journey:
Kristin Nitz, Sondy Eklund, Vicki Sansum, Kristi Lewis,
Nancy Roe-Pimm, Carol Ottolenghi, Lisa Cohn,
and Sue Moshofsky.

And to Regina Griffin and Suzanne Reinoehl
at Holiday House, who made this book possible.

CONTENTS

RUN FROM THE NUN!

Chapter 1

BREAKOUT

Kara McKinney vowed her first day at St. Joan of Arc School would be her last.

Sure, she was trapped right now, squished into the line of kids filing into the gray granite building, but not for long. She'd been planning her escape ever since her parents announced she had to switch schools. Once Kara made her getaway, she'd flash her story across the Internet for the whole world to read:

Girl Busts Out of Catholic School! the headline would scream. *Chased by five nuns, the brave Kara McKinney scaled a ten-foot wall, shimmied down a tree, and disappeared into the woods. Defying all odds, Kara returned to Bingham Elementary and was reunited with her best friend, Molly.*

The line surged forward, depositing Kara into

the school's main hallway. A bell blasted, and kids stampeded toward their homerooms. Kara glanced around. No one seemed to notice her, so she waltzed right by the fifth-grade classroom where she belonged and ducked into the girls' room.

Her heart pounded as the door slammed shut. She'd wait until the coast was clear, then she'd sneak by the principal's office, slip out the back door, and run straight to Bingham.

Pew! The smell of pine cleaner made her woozy. Kara dashed to the window for a gulp of air, spying her reflection in the mirror. She hated her school uniform, especially the white blouse with its itchy collar. But the plaid skirt wasn't bad. It reminded her of Scottish warriors she'd seen in a movie. Like Kara, they dressed in tartan kilts when they rushed into battle.

Too bad they got clobbered, she thought.

Another bell sounded. Kara hurried to the door and peeked out. Seeing no one, she began tiptoeing down the green-tiled hall. Wait—what was that noise? Kara looked down to see her loose shoelaces slapping the floor. She crammed them into her shoes and crept toward the principal's office.

Suddenly a woman's voice rang out. "What are you doing?"

Kara gasped and whirled around. The hallway was empty.

She heard a deep voice with a foreign accent coming from the principal's office. "But Sister Mary Francis, I have my list right here," said a man. "It says to start with your office."

"Stop right now, Gino!" Sister commanded.

Kara knew she should keep going, but curiosity gripped her. She'd never met Sister Mary Francis, the school principal. Maybe the nun was about to nail someone.

She peered into the room, and her eyes widened. Sister Mary Francis was taller than Kara's father, who stood six feet. She wore a nun's uniform—a dark veil, a black dress that fell to her shins, and a silver cross around her neck. Her feet didn't look like nun feet, though. Sister was sporting black tennis shoes.

"What a mess, Gino!" Sister said, pointing to newspapers spread across the floor. "Thank goodness you didn't start painting." She crumpled a paper and lobbed it across the room. *Zing!* It landed in the trash can. Score one for the nun!

Kara pictured Sister dribbling down a basketball court, making a three-point shot and waving to a cheering crowd.

Gino wasn't cheering, though. He scrambled to pick up a paint bucket. Kara checked him out: tall, tan, with dark curly hair. His white T-shirt showed off his muscles.

"I believe I asked you to paint my office last Friday, not on the first day of school," said Sister.

"I'm sorry. I must have gotten confused."

"That's understandable," said Sister. "You've taken on a lot of extra work beyond your janitorial duties."

It was time to beat it. As Kara inched forward, her new shoes squeaked loudly. In a flash, the nun's eyes were upon her.

"What do you think you're doing, young lady?"

Kara's mouth went dry. When she tried to speak, nothing came out.

"What is your name?" demanded the principal.

Kara gulped and gazed up, way up, to meet the nun's piercing stare.

"Step into my office," Sister said.

Kara turned on her heels and bolted. She pumped her arms, her breath coming in short bursts as she zoomed down the hallway. She heard the nun shout, "Come back here!" and whipped around to see Sister Mary Francis fly out of her office, her veil flapping and her cross swinging wildly.

It was just as she'd imagined: a getaway with a nun in pursuit! This was a battle of wills, a contest between the weak and the mighty. The nun had long legs, but she, Kara McKinney, had a head start.

To pick up speed, Kara tossed her backpack. She glanced over her shoulder to see a red-faced Sister leap over the backpack in a single bound. Kara nearly crashed into a statue in the hall, but recovered in time and sprinted for the exit.

The nun came pounding after her. The back door was getting closer and closer. Its brass doorknob gleamed, only inches away. Just as she reached for the door, Kara tripped over her shoelaces and fell to the floor.

Chapter 2

ATTACK OF THE MOUTH BOY

Sister Mary Francis swooped down and pulled Kara to her feet. "You can save that hundred-yard dash for Field Day—if you're not in detention, that is. Now what is your name?"

Kara clamped her mouth shut. A captured warrior should reveal nothing.

The nun studied her. "I don't recognize you, so you must be a new student. I'd say you're about ten years old, and there's only one new girl in the fifth grade. You are Kara McKinney."

Kara's jaw dropped. Sherlock Nun!

Sister pushed a strand of red hair back into her veil. "Normally, I'd give you detention for this outrageous behavior," she said sternly. "However, it's your first day in a new school, and you must be nervous. I'm willing to give you another chance, but don't disappoint me."

"Yes, Sister." Kara's eyes darted around, seeking another exit.

A long hand emerged from the deep folds of Sister's habit and grasped Kara's arm. "I'll escort you to your classroom." Sister steered Kara down the hall, retrieved her backpack, and ushered her into the fifth grade.

"Good morning, Sister Mary Francis," said the students, rising like a wave.

"Thank you, class. Please sit down." Sister turned to a young woman at the front of the room. "Miss Monet, I'd like to introduce Kara McKinney. She's delighted to join your class."

"Kara, welcome!" said Miss Monet with a warm smile. "I was afraid you got lost. I'm so glad to see you."

Kara nodded and searched for an empty desk. All the kids were staring at her. Her knees began to shake. She had to sit down, now. She spotted a desk in the back of the room and started toward it, but Miss Monet put her hand on Kara's shoulder.

"Are you new to Strafford?" asked the teacher.

"No." Kara had lived in the same Philadelphia suburb her whole life, but right now she wished she lived on Mars.

"Do you want to tell us about yourself?" Miss Monet asked.

"No, thank you," said Kara, twisting her hands and wondering if this torture would ever end.

"All right. Please sit there." Miss Monet pointed to a desk behind a skinny boy with black hair. Kara walked down the aisle, ignoring the whispers, and sank into her chair.

"Back to work, class." As Sister swept out, she brushed the blackboard and a smidge of chalk dust blotted her habit. She flicked her fingers, instantly erasing the spot.

Sister's footsteps echoed down the hall, and each thud reminded Kara that she was a prisoner. She leaned back in her chair to survey enemy territory.

Miss Monet wore a blue pantsuit, with a scarf tied loosely around her neck. She had billowing brown curls and blue eyes the color of a swimming pool. She glided down the aisles, distributing papers. Her perfume smelled like honeysuckles and summer. When she reached Kara, she bent down to whisper, "I'm new, too."

Kara smiled, but she felt an ache from deep inside. Miss Monet was so gentle, just like Kara's fourth-grade teacher at Bingham.

Bingham—that's where Molly was. Yesterday

the two girls had sworn to be best friends forever. Kara had written Molly's name on her hand, and Molly had printed *KARA* on hers. They'd used a permanent marker—metallic purple—so their names would remain forever, like their friendship.

Her mom didn't like it much, though. Mrs. Mc-Kinney had tried to scrub off the letters, but they only faded a teeny bit.

Sitting at her desk, Kara traced the wobbly *M* of Molly's name. Tears blurred her eyes, and she began to sniffle. She bent her head so her long brown hair would hide her face.

The boy in front of Kara turned around. He must have heard her sniffling!

Like all the boys at St. Joan of Arc, he wore a white shirt, gray tie, and dark blue pants. His outfit resembled the one Kara's dad wore to work.

The boy grinned, and Kara smiled tentatively. Maybe dressing up made the boys more polite here.

"Hey, new girl!" he whispered. "What's wrong with you? You look like a zombie."

Kara flinched. Before she could retort, Miss Monet rang a bell and said, "Class, please take out your math books and turn to page three."

The boy leaned closer to Kara, his dark eyes narrowing. His jowls moved up and down, and his bad

Chapter 3

A GHOSTLY GETAWAY

The soggy wad hit Kara's cheek and ricocheted past her. Kara's fingers flew to her face and found a warm, sticky spot that was Mouth Boy's slime. She leaped up, wiping her cheek furiously.

"You monster mouth!" Kara yelled. "Leave me alone!"

Miss Monet dropped her book. Everyone turned and gaped at Kara.

"Kara McKinney!" Miss Monet's eyes flashed. "Sit down immediately. We do not shout in the classroom, and we do not insult our fellow classmates."

"But he *spit* on me, Miss Monet." Kara blinked back angry tears as she plopped in her chair. She felt as if she were sitting in a huge stadium with all the lights on her. She scanned the floor for evidence, but the spitball was gone.

"I did not spit on her!" protested Mouth Boy.

Silence. Miss Monet looked from the boy to Kara and back again. She consulted her seating chart. "Anthony Russo, I'd like to hear your explanation."

"I started coughing," Anthony replied in a buttery voice. "I turned around so I wouldn't disturb the class. Maybe some spit escaped, but I didn't mean to do it."

Miss Monet frowned. "You need to apologize to Kara."

Anthony twisted around and rolled his eyes. "I'm sorry, but it was an accident."

"Accident or not, you're in detention if this happens again," said Miss Monet, scribbling in her notebook. Kara wanted to believe she wrote: *Anthony Russo, disgusting pig.* That would teach him.

Then Miss Monet said, "Kara, I know you're upset, but you need to control your temper."

Kara felt heat rising in her cheeks. She bit her lip so she wouldn't talk back.

When Miss Monet turned away, a girl across the aisle leaned over. Her face was heart-shaped, and her eyes looked sympathetic. She whispered to Kara, "I saw the whole thing. It's not your fault."

Kara smiled at Heart Face, but she still felt

terrible. Anthony was such a creep. She watched him reach into his sock and pull out a horror comic book, which he hid under his math book. Then he lifted a candy bar out of his other sock and nibbled on it.

Sighing, Kara rubbed Molly's name on her hand and stared out the window. At Bingham, she could see green playing fields. Here she had a bird's-eye view of the church graveyard. Great, she could watch dead people all day.

Wait a minute. Graveyards were spooky, but they were also good hiding places. Kara loved watching scary movies about kids hiding behind tombstones, evading ghouls of the night. Sure, it was daytime now, and the only scary creature around was Sister Mary Francis, but Kara would steer clear of her.

The cemetery was next to the playground. Perfect. At recess, she'd hide in the graveyard, then run home. She'd sob and tell her mom all about Anthony spitting on her. Her mother didn't put up with tantrums, but she couldn't bear to see Kara suffer. With any luck, Kara would be back at Bingham tomorrow.

At lunchtime, Kara joined the line of kids snaking down the hall to the cafeteria. She paused at a statue perched on a pedestal. It was a teenage saint, dressed for battle. The plaque on the pedestal read: *St. Joan of Arc, warrior saint.*

St. Joan's serene smile seemed to say, I wish you'd stick around, but if you have to go, my lips are sealed. Kara moved on, feeling stronger.

Once in the cafeteria, she chose a crowded table near the exit. When the recess bell rang, she jumped up, but a teacher blew a whistle and announced, "Seventh and eighth graders, you may go first." By the time Miss Monet called the fifth grade, the playground was packed.

Kara stood in the middle of an asphalt yard with basketball hoops and a swing set. If she ran into the cemetery now, someone would see her. She needed another hiding place.

The big green Dumpster was her best bet. Ducking behind it, Kara mapped out her escape. She'd slip by the boys playing basketball, then creep into the graveyard.

It was a great plan, until Sister Mary Francis marched up to the basketball court and planted herself there. Sister's eagle eyes would surely spot Kara if she streaked by.

"Rotten luck," Kara mumbled, leaning against the trash bin. It smelled like rotting food. A fly buzzed around her nose, and Kara swatted it. Mr.

Gino, the janitor, came by, pushing a wheelbarrow filled with plants. Kara feared he was headed to the Dumpster, but he kept going and disappeared around the front of the school.

Kara poked her head out to check on Sister's whereabouts. To her horror, someone yelled, "Yo, Kara! I see you!"

Mouth Boy! Kara flattened herself against the Dumpster, but it was too late. Anthony charged toward her, making whooping noises. His legs pummeled the pavement, and his giant mouth hung open.

And then, crash! Anthony plowed into two little girls, and they tumbled to the ground, shrieking. Anthony spun around like a windup toy. With a blast of her whistle, Sister Mary Francis ran toward the wreck.

Kara tore across the playground like a ball shot from a cannon. She flitted under the cemetery's archway, weaving past white headstones until she spotted a gray marble building, its wrought-iron door ajar. She darted inside, slammed the door, and crouched on the cold floor. Outside she heard footsteps. They were coming closer and closer.

Kara's heart thundered. She clenched her fists, ready to defend herself.

Chapter 4

GRAVE SECRETS

The door screeched open. Kara squinted, the sunlight blinding her.

"Kara!" A voice bounced off the walls of the tomb. "I know you're in here."

That voice. She'd heard it before.

Kara stood up, and her eyes adjusted. It was Heart Face.

"What are you doing?" Heart Face stepped inside, leaving the door cracked open. "You're not allowed in here. This is a mausoleum."

"What's that?" Kara looked around uneasily. Dead roses drooped in a vase filled with greenish water, and the black petals gave off a musty smell. The building's smooth walls were bare except for one filled with fancy writing.

"A mausoleum is full of dead bodies. Not just any old bodies. This one's for dead priests." Heart Face peered at an inscription on the wall. "Looks like you're standing on top of Father Mario Piccoli."

"Yikes!" Kara hopped off the holy spot.

Heart Face walked around, sniffing. "It stinks in here. Must be the decaying bodies."

"It's just those dead roses." At least, that's what Kara hoped.

Heart Face slid to the floor, stirring up a cloud of rose petals and dust. Sunlight gleamed off her red hair, and her pale skin appeared ghostly in the tomb. She smiled. "I'm Nicole Kingston. Welcome to St. Joan of Arc."

"Um, thanks." Kara plopped down, careful not to sit on the dead priest. "And thanks for being nice to me after Anthony spit on me."

"No problem. Juvenile delinquents like Anthony Russo need to be held accountable for their actions. Don't you agree?"

Nicole sounded like a judge on Court TV. "I guess so," Kara said. "What's his problem anyway?"

"Interesting you should ask. I'm drawing up a psychological profile of him."

Kara blinked. "You're drawing pictures of Anthony?"

"No, a psychological profile is a written report

on a person's family history, personality type, abnormal behavior, stuff like that."

"How'd you learn to do that?" Kara asked.

Nicole sat straighter. "My older sister's in college, and I'm studying her criminal psychology books. I've decided that's the career for me, so I'm starting with basic work, writing up profiles of troublemakers. Anthony tops my list. He defies authority, throws spitballs, and eats candy compulsively in class. I'm afraid he'll move on to more serious offenses."

Above Nicole's head, a spider scurried up the wall and slipped into its shadowy web. Kara shivered. Her hands were cold and clammy. Nicole was interesting, but more than anything, Kara wanted to go home.

"Maybe you should go back to the playground," Kara said politely. "I bet recess is almost over. I'll stay here until it's safe to run home."

Nicole didn't budge. "We get double recess on the first day of school. Why are you going home?"

"I want to go back to my old school, Bingham Elementary."

"Why'd you switch to Catholic school?"

Kara snorted. "My parents did it. They said I needed more discipline."

Nicole whisked a notebook and pen from her pocket. "Did you get expelled from Bingham?"

"No, I did not!" Kara said. "My parents transferred me here because they hated the experimental program I was in."

"Wow! Your teachers conducted experiments on you?"

"No." Kara giggled. "They weren't mad scientists or anything. It was this new program where you worked at your own pace. I signed a contract to do a bunch of work, but nobody checked on me, so I wrote my first book. It was a mystery, about a detective named Katie Lang."

"Fun. I love mysteries, too. So what happened next?"

"I had to leave Katie Lang trapped in a snake pit, with no way out, because my parents took my book away. They found out I hadn't done any math for three weeks."

"Uh-oh." Nicole was writing furiously.

Kara leaned against the wall and sighed. "Boy, were they mad. I had to do extra math, but I still got a bad grade. That's when my parents went nuts and transferred me here."

Nicole closed her notebook. "It's not so bad here. You just have to watch out for Sister Mary

Francis. She's one of those die-hard nuns who still wears a habit, and she's pretty strict."

"What about Miss Monet? Is she a nun in training?"

Nicole laughed. "No, she's a regular teacher. The church is running low on nuns. Sister Mary Francis is the only one we've got."

So much for discipline. Wait until Kara told her parents about the nun shortage.

Nicole glanced at her watch. "We should go now. Sometimes Father DiMarini visits the mausoleums."

As Nicole jumped up, a pen rolled from her pocket. She went after it, skidding across the marble floor, and knocked over the flower vase. It shattered, scattering glass fragments and rose petals.

"Oh, no." Nicole's hand flew to her mouth.

"Let's get out of here," said Kara.

The girls crept through the cemetery, heads low, Nicole in the lead. Somehow they ended up near the woods behind the graveyard.

"Oops, we went the wrong way," Nicole said. "I've never been good with directions." Suddenly she grabbed Kara's hand. "Look!"

At the edge of the graveyard, Kara saw a big hole in the ground.

"That looks suspicious," said Nicole.

"Maybe there's a funeral today."

"But this is already somebody's grave." Nicole knelt down to read a crumbling tombstone on the ground. "Actually, it's two people's graves! Joseph Ricci and his wife, Maria. They both died in 1918."

Nicole peered into the hole. "The dirt's still soft, so it's only recently been disturbed. I think somebody dug up their bodies."

"You do?" Kara squatted beside Nicole, poking gingerly through the dirt. She didn't want to touch any worms or body parts. Then she felt something and pulled it out. "Look at this."

"A Snickers wrapper!" Nicole's green eyes lit up. "That's an important clue."

"It is?"

"Only one person would eat candy while digging up bodies. Anthony Russo!"

Goose bumps ran up Kara's arms. "But why would he do that?"

"He must be more disturbed than I thought," said Nicole, shaking her head. "We're going to have to figure out his motive, then set a trap and catch him."

The recess bell rang. "Hurry, hurry!" urged Nicole. The girls flew through the cemetery, hid behind the Dumpster, and watched Sister herding kids into school.

When the nun turned her back, Kara said, "I'm outta here. I'm going home."

"Are you crazy? Sister Mary Francis will catch you for sure." Nicole yanked Kara into line. "Meet me in the graveyard tomorrow. We'll investigate some more."

"I won't be back," Kara whispered. "No way."

Chapter 5

BETRAYED

At last Kara was home. It was time to show her mom how she'd ruined Kara's life.

Her mother was in the kitchen doing yoga stretches. She was wearing a Bingham PTA T-shirt. The nerve!

"There you are, Kara!" her mother said. "So how was the new school?"

Kara didn't answer, and her mom handed her a plate. "I made your favorite brownies, the kind with black walnuts."

Kara couldn't believe it. Her mom hadn't baked in months. She must be feeling guilty about sending her to a new school. A good sign.

"No, thanks, my stomach hurts." Kara left and thumped upstairs to her bedroom. She debated whether or not to slam the door, and decided to go for it. *Wham!* She liked the noise so much, she slammed the door again. Then she fell on her bed and waited. It didn't take long.

Her mother knocked and came in. "Kara, what's wrong?"

"My life! It's ruined!"

"What happened?" said her mother, sitting beside Kara.

"A disgusting boy spit on me in front of the whole class."

"What? Who spit on you? I'll call Sister Mary Francis."

Uh-oh. Her mom would find out about Kara's run from the nun, and she'd be in big trouble.

"Never mind. He already got punished," Kara said quickly. "But guess what? Sister Mary Francis is the only nun there! What kind of a Catholic school is that? Pull me out now, and you'll get your money back."

"We don't want our money back." Her mom reached over to smooth Kara's hair. "Look, I know it's hard to go to a new school. Just give it a little time."

Kara bolted upright. "Why, so I can go to school with crazy people? Someone's digging up bodies in the graveyard!"

Her mother's brown eyes crinkled, and she laughed. "Honey, sometimes I think you should teach my creative writing class instead of me."

"I'm not making this up, Mom! Why are you doing this to me? If I can't go to Bingham, I'll never see Molly."

"You can see her after school."

"It won't be the same. We'll have different teachers, different homework, different everything. And the fifth grade at Bingham always goes skiing in the Poconos after Christmas. I've been waiting my whole life for this."

"I'll take you and Molly skiing this winter," her mother replied. "You can invite your new friends, too."

Kara flopped on her yellow pillow. "I don't want new friends!"

Her mother let out a deep sigh. "Look, Kara, I'm teaching tonight, and I have to get ready. We'll talk more later."

"By the time you get home, I'll be dead. Killed by a spitting disease."

"I hear walnut brownies are the cure," said her mom as she left the room.

Kara waited until her mother went downstairs, then she grabbed the phone in the hall, took it to her room, and dialed Molly's number.

Molly's older sister, Blair, answered right away. Blair seemed to live with the phone glued to her ear.

"Is Molly there?" Kara asked.

"Nope. She went over to some girl's house."

"What girl?"

"Um, let me think. Cheryl Valentine."

Kara nearly dropped the phone. Cheryl Valentine! That show-off. Cheryl thought she was so great because she had long blond hair and owned horses. Her high-pitched voice sounded like a horse's whinny. Molly and Kara used to avoid her.

"Oh," said Kara in a small voice. "Tell her to call me." In a daze she returned to her room. She'd been gone only one day, and already Molly had a new friend.

An image flashed through her mind: Molly and Cheryl galloping on horseback across a field, laughing and talking, with Kara running after them, calling, "Wait! Wait for me!" Suddenly the horses kicked up a cloud of dust, blinding her. Kara tripped and landed in a pile of horse poop.

"Stop, crazy thoughts!" Kara said aloud, and she dragged a shoebox from her closet. It was full of pictures of Molly and Kara, notes, letters, and other friendship stuff. Kara rooted through the box until she found a letter that Molly wrote her last year.

The letter read,

Why You Are My Best Friend

1. You make me laugh so hard, my whole body shakes.
2. You are FUN! You put on plays in your basement and invite the whole neighborhood (even Pepper Weaver). Thanks for making me STAR of your plays!
3. We go exploring together. Remember how we found that jewelry box in a field, and your mom called the police, and they said it was stolen? It was so cool when the owner gave us a reward because she was so happy to get her grandma's locket back.
4. We wear our matching purple socks every Tuesday.
5. The best thing is, we hang out, and eat M&M's and tell each other everything.

Kara sifted through the box, smiling at old photos, until someone pounded on her door.

"I'm busy," said Kara, shoving the shoebox into her closet.

The door flew open, and Molly ran into the room.

"Molly!" Kara hugged her. Molly still looked the same, with her hazel eyes and seven freckles sprinkled across her nose like the Big Dipper.

"What are you staring at?" said Molly with a grin. "And why are you still wearing your uniform?"

Kara gasped. Molly was wearing a red T-shirt and shorts, like a normal person, and here Kara was, dressed like a freak. "Don't look at me! Close your eyes!" Kara tore off her clothes and changed into jeans.

"So what happened?" asked Molly, settling onto Kara's bed.

"I almost got away, but this long-legged nun nabbed me, then a hideous Mouth Boy spit on me in front of the whole class."

"No way!" Molly's eyes widened. "That's so gross!"

"You're telling me."

"Do you have to go back?"

"For now, but I'll find another way to escape." Kara sat down beside Molly. "So tell me everything. What did I miss today?"

"Not much. Our teacher's Mr. Johnson, and our classroom has a cool mural of the rain forest with parrots and monkeys and jaguars. So what's your school like?"

Kara heaved a sigh. "First of all, it's not my school, and second, it's awful. They don't even have grass on the playground. It's all concrete, like a prison."

"Sounds terrible. Did you pray in church all day?"

"No, we did regular stuff like science and social studies and reading. But I don't want to talk about it." Kara kept her voice casual. "I just called your house. Where were you?"

"Oh, I went over to Cheryl Valentine's. Just for five minutes." Molly's left eye twitched. A sure sign she felt guilty.

Kara snorted. "What do you care about Cheryl?"

"I wanted to see her new horse, Daffodil. Cheryl says I can go riding with her someday."

"Really? How'd you end up talking to her?"

"She sat next to me on the bus."

Kara and Molly always sat together on the bus. Kara felt her chest tighten, and her voice sounded funny when it came out. "You let her sit there?"

"I didn't want to be mean. Besides, she's not so bad."

"But *I* want to sit next to you."

"You will," Molly promised. "As soon as you get back, I'll switch seats." She glanced at the clock. "I need to go. It's my turn to help with dinner."

Kara walked Molly downstairs. "Thanks for coming over," she said.

Molly ran off, and Kara trudged back to her room. She grabbed a pen and pad and sat down at her desk. At the top of the paper, she wrote: *What is a true friend?* She thought about it for a long time, until her head hurt. Finally, she realized she didn't know the answer. She folded up the paper and put it away, but the question bounced in her mind all night.

Chapter 6

CAUGHT
RED-HANDED

At school the next day, Kara sank into her seat behind Anthony, who was gnawing on a candy bar. He crossed his eyes at her. Kara stuck out her tongue.

"Hi! You're back," Nicole chirped, passing Kara a card made out of red construction paper. The cover said *Welcome, Kara!* and Nicole had sketched two smiling girls walking hand in hand through a field of flowers.

Kara grinned, until she opened the card and saw a picture of a sinister boy excavating a grave. Nicole had scrawled, *Beware of Anthony! Read my note for juicy details!*

Miss Monet was out in the hall, so Kara opened the note tucked inside the card and read:

FILE ON ANTHONY RUSSO

Personal Background: Anthony's parents own a construction company. He probably used their equipment to dig up graves. Anthony has one brother, Bruno, a star athlete in high school, and a five-year-old sister, Dina, a prizewinning tap dancer. As a middle child, Anthony may feel lost and alienated.

Theory #1: Personality type: Loner. Wants friends but doesn't know how to make them. He offends the living, so he has decided to befriend the dead. A fan of horror movies and comic books, he suffers from delusions that he can bring bodies back to life.

Theory #2: Personality type: Extrovert, show-off. In an attempt to impress everyone, he is stealing bodies so he can become a cult hero. He has a secret desire to be caught, which is why he left the candy wrapper in the open grave.

Suddenly Anthony turned around and snatched the note away.

"You give that back!" Kara demanded.

"That's private." Nicole leaped up and pinched him.

"Get your claws off me!" yelped Anthony, stuffing the paper in his pocket.

Just then Miss Monet came into the room.

"Nicole Kingston, please sit down. Class, we have a special visitor today."

A priest loomed in the doorway. It was Father DiMarini, pastor of St. Joan of Arc Church, which Kara and her family attended every Sunday. A short man with furry gray eyebrows, Father DiMarini frowned when children made too much noise in church. One look from Father DiMarini, and parents took their noisy kids outside.

Kara liked the priest because he burned tons of incense. The rich, spicy smell appealed to her. Father spoke English with a heavy accent and waved his hands like an actor when he delivered sermons. After Mass, he mingled with parishioners and spoke in Italian with the older Italian Americans.

"Good morning," said Father. "I have come to make an announcement."

Kara's classmates shifted uneasily. The room grew still except for the humming of a fan in the back.

Father's eyes roved the aisles. "Yesterday, I was in the rectory, and I looked out my window. And what did I see? Two little girls playing in the cemetery."

Kara's stomach clenched in fear. Father DiMarini seemed to be staring right at her.

"They violated the sanctuary of the dead," he intoned. "They entered a crypt holding the remains of our dearly departed priests. Later I searched the tomb, and I saw glass all over." Father waved his hands, knocking an eraser off the board. "A vase of roses, smashed!"

Kara thought she was going to faint.

The priest moved closer, his black cassock rustling across the floor. "I am tired of telling you students to stay out of the cemetery." He shook his finger. "If I catch you in the graveyard, I will kick you out of school!"

Kara bolted upright. It was a miracle—her ticket out! She was about to shout, "It was me! It was me!" when she glanced at Nicole. The color had drained from Nicole's face, and she was chewing on her fingernails.

If Kara told, she might get Nicole in trouble, too.

"I will hear confessions tomorrow," said Father. "It is good to start the school year with the holy sacrament of confession. Perhaps those two girls will want to clean their consciences."

Normally Kara didn't mind going to confession; it felt good to get sins off her chest. But this time she had an accomplice.

The students were so quiet Kara could hear a clock ticking. Finally Father murmured a blessing and slipped away. Kara wanted to tear after him, but first she had to talk to Nicole.

At lunchtime recess, Kara grabbed Nicole and pulled her over to the Dumpster so they could talk in private.

"Are you going to confess?" Kara asked.

"No," replied Nicole. "I'm not going to confession."

"But you have to! It's one of those church rules."

"I'm not Catholic," said Nicole.

"You aren't Catholic? Then what are you doing in Catholic school?" Kara asked in disbelief.

"You don't have to be Catholic to go here," Nicole said. "Most kids are, but not everyone. My parents picked this school because classes are smaller."

Kara retorted, "Well, I'm going to confess. I have to."

Nicole grasped Kara's arm. "No, you don't. You can take the Fifth Amendment. You have the right not to incriminate yourself."

"What?"

"You don't have to give information that makes you look guilty."

"Look, we aren't in court," said Kara.

"Not yet." Nicole began pacing. "If no one confesses, Father might launch an investigation. Suspects would be rounded up, and Sister Mary Francis might finger us. I think she saw us running in late yesterday."

"That won't happen."

"Please don't tell!" pleaded Nicole. "Father will ask you who was with you. I don't want to get kicked out of school! I've gone here my whole life."

"I won't rat on you," Kara assured her.

"But he'll make you. I've heard there's a secret tunnel connecting the church to the rectory. I bet the priests have a room in the rectory where they question the really bad sinners."

Kara rolled her eyes. Kids were always spreading stories that you could go into a confessional and never come out, but it was just a stupid rumor. At least, she hoped so.

Then she remembered Father's warning: "If I catch you in the graveyard, I will kick you out of school." Maybe she didn't have to go to confession. She could run into the cemetery right now and refuse to leave. The priest would march outside and expel her.

"Come on, Kara, we have more important things to worry about," Nicole coaxed. "For starters, we need to crack the grave-digging case."

Kara shook her head. "Nicole, I want to help you, but I have to confess, and I have to do it now." With that, Kara lit across the playground.

Nicole shouted, "Stop!" but Kara kept going, zipping by the boys playing basketball and dodging a game of red rover until she reached the entry to the graveyard.

Then she stopped short, because Mr. Gino was blocking her path.

"Where are you going?" The janitor frowned.

Kara squeaked, "Um, I'm visiting my dead aunt." Pretty lame, but the best she could do under the circumstances.

"You're not allowed in there without an adult." Mr. Gino's dark eyebrows furrowed into a jagged line, and he waved his hand. "Now go play."

Anger surged through Kara, and she charged forward, darting around Mr. Gino. She didn't see the shovel on the ground until she tripped. The janitor caught her before she fell on her face.

"Enough games. Go back to school," he said.

Kara fled. She thought she heard Mr. Gino chuckling, an eerie sort of laughter.

She made it to the school entrance as the bell pealed, and leaned against the door, gasping. She'd better get out of this school, and fast.

Chapter 7

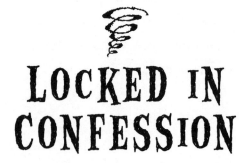

LOCKED IN CONFESSION

That evening, Kara tried calling Molly to tell her what had happened.

Molly's sister reported, "Sorry, she's spending the night at our aunt Sue's." Kara couldn't help but wonder if Molly was really at Cheryl Valentine's.

Later she tossed in bed, having nightmares about confession, graveyards, and Cheryl. The next day, bleary-eyed, Kara left a note under her pillow: *Dear Mom and Dad, I'm going to confession. If I don't come back, search the rectory. I might be locked up for questioning. Please rescue me. Your daughter, Kara.*

When she got to school, Miss Monet told the class they were going to church for confession.

"Those who aren't Catholic will have quiet time in the church, while the others go to confession."

As Kara and her classmates shuffled over to the church, Nicole sidled up to her and whispered, "What are you going to do?"

"Sh," Kara said anxiously.

"You won't tell on me, will you?"

"Swear."

Kara mounted the steep stone steps leading into the church, which smelled of smoky incense and burning candles. She dipped her hand in a font of holy water and crossed herself. The cool water felt good on her sweaty forehead. Her classmates divided into two lines in the center aisle.

Two lines meant that two priests were hearing confessions. Not knowing which confessional Father DiMarini was in, Kara spotted Molly's name on her left hand. Maybe that was a sign. She squeezed into the left line.

Kara lifted her eyes to the church's stained-glass windows, with pictures of angels and saints, and she silently prayed, Please help me, God, and make this go fast!

Someone poked her. She turned to see Nicole behind her.

"What are you doing?" murmured Kara. She

looked for Miss Monet, but the teacher was several rows away, her head bent in prayer.

"I found out Father DiMarini and Father Benedict are hearing confessions. Now listen." Nicole pointed to a girl with blond hair at the front of the line. "Claire's going to help you. She'll signal when she gets out of confession. If she scratches her nose, she had Father DiMarini. You can switch lines, and you won't have to confess."

But Kara wanted Father DiMarini. He had the power to free her. She watched as Claire entered the confessional. She was in there forever.

"I should have picked someone with a cleaner record," grumbled Nicole.

Finally, Claire emerged, scratching her nose. "Quick! Switch now!" said Nicole.

"Leave me alone," Kara hissed.

Miss Monet materialized beside them. "Quiet, girls. Nicole, sit down right now."

The line moved forward. At last it was Kara's turn. She lifted the creaky lock on the door, then stepped into the tiny dark confessional and knelt on a bench covered with red velvet.

A wall with a screen separated her from the priest, but Kara could see Father DiMarini's shadow. She stammered, "Bless me, Father, for I have sinned. It's been three months since my last confession."

"Yes, my child. Tell me your sins."

Kara traced her fingers along the paneled wall, trying to find a secret door to the rectory like Nicole said. In the meantime, she needed a sin, fast.

"I have mean thoughts about this boy. He spit on me, and he's a big liar, too."

"The Lord will deal with him. We are here to talk about you."

No sign of a secret door, so Kara summoned her courage. "There is one thing—"

"Yes?"

"It was me you saw in the graveyard!"

"Ah!" The priest let out a deep breath. "Why did you go in there? You and your friend, you were playing hide-and-seek on holy ground."

"No, it wasn't like that," said Kara. She bit her lip, then went on, "Breaking the flower vase was an accident, but I shouldn't have gone in there. I deserve to be punished. Severely punished."

She bowed her head, thrilled with her confession. Silence.

"Father? Did you hear me?"

"You are forgiven. Stay out of the graveyard and say the rosary. Now go in peace."

Kara nearly fell over. "I'm forgiven?" Her voice began to rise. "But you said you'd kick me out of school if you caught me in the graveyard!"

"I didn't catch you. Instead, you came to tell me."

"But, Father, you promised—"

"I lost my temper. Besides, this confession is confidential. Even if you are a murderer, I can't tell anyone. It's a vow we take as priests. I'll go to my grave with the secret."

Kara stood up, shaking with fury, and twisted the doorknob. The lock was jammed. She was trapped in here! Kara slammed her foot into the door.

"Watch it!" warned the priest. The door flew open, and a hand yanked Kara out. It was Nicole, her face lined with worry. Kara looked for Miss Monet, but her teacher was up at the altar.

Nicole hustled Kara down the church steps. "Are you all right? Did you confess?"

"Yes, I did, and he told me to say the rosary," spat Kara.

"Wow, fifty Hail Marys and ten Our Fathers. That'll take you all day." Nicole drew a sharp breath. "After you say it, then you're kicked out?"

"No! He forgave me! The rosary is my penance, then everything is all right."

Nicole froze in the church courtyard. "Did he ask for my name?"

"No. He didn't even want to know *my* name."

"Oh, Kara, I'm so happy! We're safe! We're free!" Nicole twirled her around.

Kara shook herself loose. Waves of disappointment washed over her, and tears trickled down her cheeks. She had failed at her most important mission.

Nicole said slowly, "I get it. You *wanted* to get kicked out, didn't you?"

"Yessss. My best friend is at Bingham. Only she might not be my best friend for long. This other girl is trying to steal her."

"That's too bad." Nicole squeezed Kara's hand. "I know how you feel. Claire Daniels—she's the girl who helped us. Well, she used to be my best friend."

"What happened?"

"Everything changed this summer. I discovered criminals, and Claire discovered boys."

"Huh?"

Nicole grinned. "See, my parents went out of town for a week, and they put my older sister Jeannine in charge of me. She didn't want to miss class, so she snuck me into her criminology class. Her professor used to be a prison psychologist. When Dr. Trgovac talked about analyzing criminals and catching them, I got chills all over. But when I tried to tell Claire about it, she just wanted to go to the pool and look at boys."

"So you aren't friends anymore?"

"Oh, we still talk, but she hangs out with Monica Nunziata now."

Other kids were streaming out of church, so the girls picked up their pace and headed back to school. Kara muttered, "I can't believe I have to go back."

"Maybe you'll like it here one of these days," said Nicole. "I want you to stay. You're the only one who can help me expose Anthony."

Kara said quickly, "Thanks, but I really want to go back to my old school. We can still be friends, though."

"Well, okay." Nicole paused at the school entrance and locked eyes with Kara. "I don't want you to be sad. If you have to go, I'll help you."

"I don't want to get you in trouble. I can do this by myself."

"Face it, you need help," Nicole said. "Two minds are better than one."

Kara thought Nicole had some crazy ideas in that mind of hers. Still, a crazy idea was better than no ideas at all, and Kara was running on empty.

"Okay," she said. "But we need to work really fast."

"Just think of me as your partner in crime," said Nicole, giving Kara a high five.

Kara grinned and said, "Okay, partner."

Chapter 8

REBEL
WITH A CAUSE

A few days later, Kara was right back where she'd started—hiding in the girls' rest room. But this time Nicole stood at her side.

"Are you ready?" Nicole demanded.

"Prepared for battle," said Kara. She unzipped her backpack and pulled out her secret weapon: her father's black Aerosmith T-shirt. Her father called it a sacred shirt, and he kept it preserved in a special box in his closet.

Kara pulled on the garment and rolled up the sleeves. A shiver ran through her body, not a scary shiver, but a surge of power. Next she took off her blue kneesocks and donned striped black tights and clunky clogs.

"Great! You look like a social misfit," said Nicole, digging around in her backpack. "Here, I brought my sister's makeup. It's illegal here." She rubbed red blush on Kara's cheeks until she looked like a clown, then she pulled out a lipstick. "And you can wet your lips with Forbidden Fruit."

Kara rolled it on, smacking her lips and savoring the raspberry taste.

"And now the crowning glory. Glitter Glow eye shadow. It's so fluorescent, your eyes will look like an alien's. My sister's running low, so I put a little water in it."

Kara dipped her fingers into the container of gooey pink eye shadow and smeared it up to her brows. To her horror, a bright blob fell on her shirt.

"Oh, no!" she cried. Makeup on the sacred shirt!

Nicole ran over to the sink and splashed water on Kara. The stain spread all over, casting a shimmery glow.

"I'm dead!" Kara said.

The bell rang. "I have to go," said Nicole. "We'll fix the shirt later."

Kara sat on a toilet seat and stared at her watch. When three minutes passed, she strutted down the hall and into the fifth grade, planting herself before the class like a tree.

"It's too early for Halloween!" Anthony roared. Everybody hooted.

Miss Monet put her hands on her hips. "Kara, what are you doing?"

"I don't like wearing a uniform," replied Kara.

"You can't come to school like that," called out Nicole. "What an outrage!"

Miss Monet walked over and said, "Is this some type of joke?"

Kara shook her head.

"Throw her out of school!" clamored Nicole.

Miss Monet's face turned pink, the exact shade of the grapefruit Kara's mother ate each morning. "Kara, go see Sister Mary Francis. And Nicole, I'll see you after class."

Kara rocketed toward the principal's office, nearly crashing into the statue of St. Joan of Arc. St. Joan seemed to give her a disapproving look. Kara would be glad to get back to Bingham, where statues didn't keep an eye on things.

Sister Mary Francis's eyebrows flew up when she saw Kara. "You have detention. After school today."

Kara had to do better than detention. She stuck out her chin and proclaimed, "I won't wear my uniform. Ever."

Sister stood up from behind her massive oak desk. "You're not the first person to defy our dress code, but your outfit is the most ridiculous. I'll call your parents, and we will put an end to this nonsense. Now where is your uniform?"

"I left it at home." Kara's stomach fluttered.

"Lying will not help."

"I'm a liar, a deviant, and a rebel." Kara repeated the words Nicole had coached her to say.

"I think some time in detention will address your character flaws. Where is your uniform?"

Kara's shoulders drooped. "In the trash can in the girls' room," she said.

"Retrieve it at once, wash off that ridiculous makeup, and report to me at three o'clock."

Back in her classroom, clad in her wrinkled uniform, Kara lowered her head to avoid gawking students. When lunchtime came, everyone hurried to their lockers to grab their lunches, but Nicole held Kara back to ask what happened.

"I only scored detention," Kara grumbled.

"Rats! So breaking the dress code is only a misdemeanor."

Miss Monet stood at the door, calling out, "Girls, hurry up." Just then the classroom phone rang, and Miss Monet went back into the room.

As the girls sped to their lockers, Nicole grabbed Kara's hand. "Look! Anthony left his locker open."

Kara felt a thrill of excitement when she saw the locker was ajar. "He must have been in a big rush to eat his desserts."

"We've got to search it," Nicole whispered frantically.

"Hurry. Miss Monet could show up any minute."

While Kara maintained surveillance, Nicole opened the locker and gasped. "He's got a shovel in there. And mud-caked boots."

Kara shivered. "What else?"

"A stack of comic books, the Walking Dead series."

They heard Miss Monet's footsteps, so Nicole shut Anthony's locker, and the girls scampered down the hall. "It won't be long before this case is closed," Nicole crowed.

"Now you just have to close *my* case," said Kara.

Afternoon classes usually dragged like a funeral, but today, with detention looming, the hours passed in a blur. Soon Kara found herself back in the office watching Sister Mary Francis open a manila file labeled *Kara McKinney*.

A good sign. The nun had a file on her.

Sister motioned for Kara to sit down. "I contacted your father at work."

Kara gulped. Her dad freaked out when he got calls from school. He always thought someone had died.

"Imagine how distressed he was to learn what happened today." Sister shook her head. "Especially when he heard about the Aerosmith T-shirt."

Kara stared at the floor and squirmed.

"Your father and I discussed your unhappiness about being here. Your parents want to make this work, and so do I, but you cannot flout the rules. Do you understand?"

"Yes, Sister."

"Which leads to your detention. The school newsletters must go out, and you will label them. You and Anthony Russo, that is." These last words fell like a dropped plate.

"What?" Kara squeaked.

"Anthony has detention today, too. I caught him trying to sneak into the graveyard at recess. I got mud all over my new Nikes chasing him."

"Please, Sister, let me do something else," Kara begged. "I'll empty trash cans, I'll clean toilets, I'll do anything but work with Anthony."

"The newsletters must go out," said Sister relentlessly. "You'll work in the office until four o'clock, when your father will pick you up. Now if you'll excuse me, I have a meeting."

With a shudder, Kara headed across the hall to the main office. Detention with Anthony Russo. Nothing could be worse.

Chapter 9

DOING TIME

Anthony sat at a long wooden table, munching on a candy bar. A glob of marshmallow cream oozed down his chin and fell to the floor. He swiped it up, licked his fingers, then smacked his lips.

Kara's stomach heaved as she plunked down at the table. Anthony tossed her a stack of newsletters and said, "Welcome to the child labor camp."

Thwack! Kara slapped on labels as fast as she could. It felt great to pound something.

Anthony said, "I can't believe I'm stuck here. There's a full moon tonight, and I've got a lot to do." He grinned at Kara, and she gulped. Only grave robbers worked by the full moon.

"So what's this newsletter about, anyway?" she said, avoiding his eyes.

Propping his feet on the table, Anthony opened a newsletter and read: " 'St. Joan of Arc School to celebrate seventy-fifth anniversary next month! Please attend our anniversary celebration on October sixth for parents, alumni, and honored guests.' "

Anthony snorted. "Why brag about this dump? We need a new school, one with air-conditioning and a swimming pool."

Kara shrugged.

"Here's another newsflash," said Anthony. " 'Sister Mary Francis and Miss Monet will attend a national conference in Florida about Catholic schools.' " He rolled his eyes. "I bet they're going to Disneyworld. Well, at least they'll be gone a few days."

Kara perked up. With Miss Monet and Sister out of town, maybe she could escape.

"This thing is BORING. I need some air." Anthony cranked open a window and whistled. "Look! There's Mr. Gino in the graveyard!"

Kara ran over and spotted Mr. Gino at the edge of the cemetery, pushing a wheelbarrow filled with a lumpy sack. She saw a glint of something silver, maybe a shovel. Mr. Gino wore a black sweatshirt with the hood pulled up. He glanced both ways, then disappeared into the woods behind the graveyard.

"So what's the big deal?" Kara asked.

"Look, I read Nicole's note. You guys think I'm digging up graves." Anthony threw back his head, cackling. "You kill me."

Kara inched toward the door, prepared to run. If only she had this on tape.

"I decided I'd creep you out, maybe hide in that hole and jump out when you and Nicole came back. So I started watching the cemetery, and I noticed Mr. Gino hanging out there and slinking into the woods. He's a janitor, so what's he doing back there? I tried tailing him at recess, but Sister nabbed me."

"You're trying to throw us off," said Kara. "We have evidence. Nicole and I searched your locker and saw a shovel and the *Walking Dead* comic books."

"I knew you'd look! I put that there to mess with you guys. Forget about me. You need to focus on Mr. Gino."

"Oh, he's just pulling weeds."

"What are you, Little Red Riding Hood? Wake up and smell the dead bodies."

Kara sniffed. "I'll share this information with Nicole. She's in charge of the investigation."

"You can't ditch me," Anthony said. "If we can catch Mr. Gino stealing bodies, the police will be all over this, and we'll get a big reward. I want my share."

Kara ignored him. She sat down to finish the newsletters while Anthony read a comic book. Finally, the hands of the clock moved to four o'clock.

"Free at last!" Anthony zipped out the door.

Kara sprinted into the hall, hoping to avoid her father. It was not her lucky day. The front door banged open, and her father hurried inside. His blond hair looked windswept, and his tie was askew. "Well, young lady, I hear you were in fine form today," he began.

"Dad, I don't know what that nun told you, but . . ."

Sister Mary Francis bounded into the hall. Her smile was so bright, Kara blinked. It must be a special smile for parents.

"Hello, Mr. McKinney." She pumped his hand. "It's nice to see you again."

"Thank you, Sister. I'm sorry about Kara's conduct today. It won't happen again."

"I'm sure it won't. We're all working hard to help Kara adjust." Sister escorted them to the door.

Kara climbed into her dad's car. He said in a chilly voice, "You have a lot of explaining to do. But first, where's my Aerosmith shirt?"

Kara ducked her head. It was going to be a long, long night.

Chapter 10

RUBBED OUT

Kara was grounded after school. No TV, no phone, no visits from Molly.

At school the next day, Kara pleaded, "Nicole, you've got to help me." The two girls were sitting on a bench at recess, having tired of swatting flies near the Dumpster.

"I will," Nicole said. "But first, what happened in detention?"

"Guess who was there?" Kara wished for a drumroll. "Anthony Russo!"

"Did you grill him? Did he say anything bizarre? Did he confess?"

"I don't think Anthony is our man," Kara said.

"What? Why not?"

Kara lifted her chin and announced, "We have a new suspect—Mr. Gino!"

"The janitor?" Nicole's eyes nearly popped.

Kara reported how she'd seen Mr. Gino wheel a mysterious bag into the woods, and how Anthony had spied him in the cemetery and woods several times.

"Clearly, Anthony's trying to frame him," said Nicole. "We've got evidence."

"Anthony claims he planted the shovel and comic books to spook us. The candy wrapper could link him to the crime scene, but maybe there's another explanation," Kara said. "Mr. Gino does act suspiciously. Plus, he's got muscles to dig up graves. Anthony's really scrawny."

"You may be on to something, McKinney," mused Nicole. "Who would ever suspect the school janitor?"

"By the way, Anthony wants in on this investigation. He thinks he'll get a big cash reward."

"No way!" Nicole's eyes shot poison arrows. "This is our case and we're not teaming up with a juvenile delinquent who remains a suspect. But I'll get to work on this new lead, pronto."

At home, Kara passed her time writing a play, *St. Kara, Heroine of Our Times*, the story of a girl who dies while saving her best friend from being trampled by wild horses. She couldn't wait to read it to Molly.

Luckily, by Friday, Kara's father pardoned her, and she was allowed to invite Molly to spend the night. That evening, the girls huddled in the family room, munching on M&M's and slurping sodas. Malabar, the family dog, snoozed beside them.

Molly sang out, "I've got a surprise."

"What is it?"

"Cheryl's dad is selling one of her horses, and my parents are buying it for me. Just think, I'll have my own horse, and you can go riding with me."

Molly jabbered on and on about her horse. How soft Star's mane was. How fast Star ran. How much Star pooped. Now that was gross. And every other word was Cheryl this and Cheryl that. When Kara couldn't stand it anymore, she interrupted.

"Molly, I need to ask you something. I'm still your best friend, aren't I?"

"Sure you are." Molly reached over to pet Malabar. It was then that Kara saw her hand.

"What happened to my name?" she cried. Kara and Molly had written each other's names only two weeks ago. The ink was supposed to be permanent, but to be safe, Kara hadn't washed her left hand. Molly's hand was smooth and clean.

"Oh, my mom rubbed it off," Molly said. "It's no big deal."

A knot formed in Kara's stomach, but she didn't say anything.

"Listen, are you ever coming back to Bingham?" Molly asked. "We're already planning the ski trip. Cheryl wants to be my roommate, but I'm not making any promises."

"I'll be back—don't worry," Kara said. She drank her soda, trying to think of a good reason for the delay. "Things are taking a little longer than I expected, because I've been investigating a possible crime at St. Joan of Arc."

"A crime?" Molly almost spit out her drink. "What kind?"

"Someone is digging up bodies in the church graveyard. I'm working on the case with Nicole. She's a very good friend of mine."

"Why would someone steal dead bodies?"

"We don't know yet," Kara said. "That's why I'm sticking around, to help Nicole with the investigation. It could break any day now."

"Nothing that exciting ever happens at Bingham," said Molly, plopping on the couch. "You still want to come back, don't you, Kara?"

"Sure I do. And put me down for your ski trip roommate."

The girls talked and watched movies late into the night.

The next morning, Molly went galloping off to a riding lesson, and Kara stomped upstairs to her bedroom. She'd wanted Molly to read her play, *St. Kara,* but Molly was too busy for her.

Her mom came in. "Want to talk?"

"No."

"Did something go wrong when Molly was here?"

"Everything's wrong," Kara said. "She's different now. She has a new friend and a new horse. I bet she wouldn't have changed if I'd stayed at Bingham."

Her mom said softly, "People change, and friendships change, but that doesn't mean Molly doesn't like you anymore."

Kara replied, "Soon she'll forget all about me unless you let me go back."

Her mother stood up. "We are not going to rehash this subject. I want you to settle down and get some rest. I'll check on you later."

Kara burrowed under her yellow comforter. She lifted her hand, the one with Molly's name on it, and rested it on her cheek as she fell into a troubled sleep.

Chapter 11

OPPORTUNITY STRIKES!

On Monday morning, Kara tried to buzz by Sister Mary Francis's office, but the nun called out, "Kara, step in here, please."

Kara went inside and saw a girl standing beside Sister.

"You aren't the only new girl in the fifth grade anymore," said Sister. "This is Marisa Yumzetti. She and her family have just moved here. I've already taken her sisters to their classrooms, but I'd like you to escort Marisa."

"Yes, Sister." Kara glanced at Marisa. She was pretty, with olive skin, shiny black hair, and big brown eyes. She looked scared. Probably she didn't want to be here.

Kara wanted to whisper, I know your pain, Marisa. But if Sister overheard, she'd be in hot water.

"I hope you two can help each other out," said Sister.

Kara nodded and led Marisa off. The new girl didn't say a word, and Kara felt tongue-tied, too. Once they reached their class, Miss Monet took over and got Marisa settled.

Midway through the morning, Sister Mary Francis marched into Kara's classroom, her face bright and rosy.

"Good morning, class! I want to talk to you about a special event next month. As you may know, we're celebrating our school's seventy-fifth anniversary and—"

"We're going to PARTY!" bellowed Anthony.

Sister's lips twitched. "It's nice to see your enthusiasm, Anthony, but that's not what I had in mind. We'll have an open house, with an exciting program for parents and guests."

Claire Daniels's hand shot up. "Are any movie stars coming?"

"None that we know of, but we're expecting the archbishop, the mayor, and some media as well."

"Cool! Will we be on TV?" asked Claire.

"Yes, BEST-TV is coming, and the cable access channel will carry our event," said Sister.

Everybody clapped and started talking all at once.

Nicole raised her voice above the din. "What kind of activities have you planned, Sister?" Her voice sounded too sweet, thought Kara, instantly on alert.

"All kinds of wonderful things. And I have a very special job for your class. You'll be in charge of a community service project."

"What's the project?" asked Nicole.

Sister smiled. "Something that reflects the spirit of our patron saint, Joan of Arc, who served God with all of her heart. We will launch a food drive to feed the hungry!"

"You mean we'll collect canned goods and stuff?" Anthony asked.

Sister nodded. "Yes, and we'll get the whole school involved!"

"That sounds like a lot of work," Claire Daniels ventured to say.

"Work?" Sister raised her eyebrows. "Joan of Arc certainly didn't shrink from a challenge."

"That's right," said Nicole. "She was such an awesome teenager. She shattered stereotypes of girls in the Middle Ages. The English invaded her country, and even the French soldiers couldn't get rid of them. So God picked Joan to kick them out. Girl power! Joan put together a whole army and won lots of battles."

Sister declared, "Now we will fight the battle to feed the hungry."

"Joan of Arc was burned at the stake," Anthony said. "Everyone thought she was a witch."

Nicole frowned. "She wasn't a witch. She was a warrior! And the church made her a saint."

"And if she were here, Anthony, she would join our crusade," Sister responded. "Now back to the food drive. Miss Monet has agreed to be the adviser, and we need a special student to lead this effort. Someone who understands the importance of our work."

A voice rang out. "I nominate Kara McKinney!"

Kara listened in horror as Nicole went on, "Kara loves to organize things. She'll do a great job."

Kara tried to object, but her tongue stuck to her mouth, and all that came out was a pathetic squeak.

"An excellent suggestion," said Sister. "Any other nominations?"

A few moments passed. Everybody stared at the floor.

"Kara, I appoint you chair of the food drive," said Sister Mary Francis. Kids cheered and pounded their desks. Kara's face flamed.

Miss Monet walked to the blackboard, her heels tapping out a rhythm that seemed to say, "Kara, you're trapped." The teacher wrote: *Kara McKinney, Chair.*

"We need a slogan for our food drive," Sister said. "Class, let's hear your suggestions."

"But—but—" Kara sputtered.

No one paid any attention. Kids started calling out ideas, and Miss Monet wrote them on the board. Just then a note landed on Kara's desk.

Kara slid the note into her lap before Anthony could steal it. She read Nicole's frantic scribbling: *DO IT! You can ruin the food drive. Steal all the food. Let Sister Mary Francis catch you. She'll kick you out, no doubt about that!*

Sabotage the food drive! Clearly, Nicole had read too many criminology books. Then again, maybe Kara didn't have to *wreck* the food drive. She could do something to make Sister Mary Francis really mad, but nothing so bad that it couldn't be fixed after she was expelled.

She heard Sister announce, "We have a great slogan. 'Live Your Faith! Feed the Hungry!' "

Miss Monet put down her chalk and said, "Kara, you haven't said a word. You do want to chair the food drive, don't you?"

"Yes," said Kara loudly. "I do."

Miss Monet gave her a warm smile. "Wonderful. Let's have some other volunteers."

"Put me down!" shouted Anthony. "I want to fight hunger!"

Kara glared at him, imagining him rooting through the charity food, his fingers snatching candy bars, and his giant lips dripping with syrup from the can of peaches he would no doubt pry open.

"Thank you, Anthony," Miss Monet said. "Anyone else?"

Kara whispered, "Pssst, Nicole," but her friend's eyes were glued to her desk.

"I'll do it," said a soft voice from across the room. It was Marisa Yumzetti.

"Thank you, Marisa. It's great to see you get involved," Sister said. She left the room, calling back, "Good luck, class!"

Miss Monet said briskly, "Kara and company, let's meet at recess."

"Hey, no one said anything about missing recess," muttered Anthony. Kara was thinking the same thing.

When the lunchtime recess bell rang, Kara grabbed Nicole's hand.

"I have to talk to you," she whispered. She found Marisa and asked, "Would you tell Miss

Monet I'll be right there? I have to use the rest room."

Then she hauled Nicole to the girls' room, threw up her hands and said, "Nicole, you promised to help me!"

"I am. I came up with the idea to ruin the food drive."

"But I need you on the committee!"

Nicole leaned against the radiator. "I'll be your adviser, but I can't be on the committee. There will be lots of meetings and stuff, and I won't be able to do my work."

"What work?"

"You know—Mr. Gino," said Nicole. "I've been nosing around. I found out he showed up here last spring, claiming he was from some town in Italy, but he says it's too small to find on any map. Suspicious, huh?"

Kara pressed her lips into a thin line.

"And get this! Nobody knows his last name. Mr. Gino says it's too long and hard to pronounce. I bet that's a cover story so he can hide out from the international police."

Kara felt a stab in her heart. Nicole cared more about catching Mr. Gino than helping her.

"Please, Kara, don't be mad." Nicole touched her arm.

"Just forget it," said Kara.

Nicole explained, "I'm trying to protect people from a serial body snatcher. I need to get that man locked up."

"Why, so you can go on TV and be a star or something?"

"Are you saying I have delusions of grandeur?" said Nicole, her face reddening to match the color of her hair.

"You bet!" Kara hoped it was some sort of insult.

"Well, you're a narcissist!"

"And what does that mean?"

"It means you're selfish!" Nicole said. "All you think about is leaving here, when some people want you to stay." Then she ran out, banging the door behind her and leaving Kara speechless.

Chapter 12

FRIENDSHIP PAIN

Kara tried not to think about the fight, but she could hardly concentrate during the food drive meeting, and later she got a bad headache. It didn't go away, even when she went home after school and rested.

At the dinner table, Kara slumped in her chair. Her mother said in a light voice, "Did anything special happen today?"

"Um, nothing much," mumbled Kara.

"That's not what I heard from Sister Mary Francis." Her mom smiled.

Kara almost choked on a clump of noodles. "What? She called you?"

"Yes, she did. I was so pleased to hear that you're in charge of the school's food drive."

Her father put down his fork and stared at his daughter. "Kara, did you get in more trouble at school? Is this some type of punishment?"

"Dad! How can you say that?"

"I thought the good Sister might be burying you in charitable work to keep you out of trouble," said her father.

"That's very uncharitable of you," said Kara in a haughty voice. "My classmates nominated me to chair the food drive."

Her mother broke in. "I'm very proud of you, honey. I think the food drive is a great idea. A lot of families need a helping hand."

Kara squirmed. It wasn't like she knew any poor people. Not personally.

"I'm sorry, sweetie." Her dad reached over to squeeze Kara's hand. "I'm glad to see you're getting into the swing of things."

"Thanks." Kara couldn't look at her parents. She finished her dinner in silence, then went to her room, saying she had to work on the food drive.

Instead, Kara climbed into bed. Her whole body ached. Her head, her stomach, even her toes. She'd heard of growing pains, but this was something else. It was friendship pain, and nothing hurt worse.

Chapter 13

SURPRISING
REVELATION

At recess the next day, Sister Mary Francis summoned Kara to her office.

"Miss Monet and I are leaving for a conference this afternoon, and we'll be gone a few days. I'm sorry we have to go right when the food drive is kicking off, but I'm sure you'll get things off to a good start. Did Miss Monet give you a list of tasks to do?"

Kara nodded. Miss Monet had given her the list, along with a peppy talk about Kara being a leader and setting a fine example for other students.

"Good. You'll have a substitute teacher who can help with publicity and anything else."

Kara suppressed a grin. She wouldn't have to

worry about a substitute interfering with her food drive. Subs were busy enough trying to control the classroom.

"Okay," Kara said. "Marisa's working on the publicity right now."

"Great. I've done a little work of my own." The nun opened a closet, took out a pole, and unfurled a white banner that read, *Live Your Faith! Feed the Hungry!*

"It looks great." Kara took the banner and placed it on the floor.

Just then Mrs. Shuey, the school secretary, walked in. "Sister, here's your ticket. And I booked that excursion for you to see the shrine of Mary, Queen of the Universe, in Orlando."

"Wonderful!" said Sister. A peaceful look passed over her face. "I love visiting shrines. You can't imagine the feeling of awe, the sense that miracles are happening all over." She sighed. "But traveling takes time and money, and that's something I don't have much of."

If Kara had money, she would pay Sister to kick her out of school.

Sister turned to Mrs. Shuey. "By the way, have you seen Mr. Gino? I'd like him to hang this banner in the hall."

"He's planting bushes in the graveyard," said Mrs. Shuey. "I don't know why he's planting shrubs where no one can see them. No one alive, that is."

Trying to cover his tracks, thought Kara.

"Never mind," said Sister. "I'll get a ladder and do it myself."

As Kara was leaving, Marisa scooted into the office. "Hi," she said shyly. "I need some help with the posters. Sister, would it be okay if Kara and Anthony and I stayed after school to work on them?"

"Certainly. Do whatever it takes, as long as you're done by four-thirty, when Mr. Gino locks up."

"I can't stay," said Kara. "My mom likes me to come straight home after school." But that wasn't the real reason. Last night, she'd called Molly and poured out her worries. Molly had invited her to come over after school to talk more.

Sister said, "Mrs. Shuey can call your mother to tell her you'll be home late. Okay?"

Kara nodded glumly. Maybe she could make it to Molly's after the meeting.

At three o'clock, Kara sat in a semicircle with Anthony and Marisa. She took out Miss Monet's list.

"Let's go over these jobs before we work on the posters," said Kara. "We need a volunteer to coordinate with all the classrooms. I'll do that." Kara would cart all the donations to Sister's office and bury her in canned peaches and beans.

"I'll help you," said Marisa. "Hey, let's brainstorm how we can get everyone excited about the food drive. Maybe we could have a contest and give away prizes."

Anthony snorted. "What's the prize, a lunch of SpaghettiOs with Sister Mary Francis?"

Kara shot Anthony a dirty look. "Let's stick to our list for now. Here's another job: work with Mr. Gino to collect boxes for food storage."

"I'm in on anything connected to Mr. Gino," said Anthony.

"You're the man for the job," said Kara. "Here's something we can all do. Stack and sort the donations."

"Did anybody donate candy yet?" asked Anthony.

"No," replied Marisa. "Besides, we're asking people to bring staples, like canned vegetables and macaroni and cereal. Not candy."

Folding up her list, Kara said, "That's it. Now we can work on the posters."

"Gotta go," said Anthony. "I have better things to do."

"Better than helping the poor?" asked Marisa. "What if you were poor and didn't have any food?"

The room grew still. Kara felt a funny burning in her throat. She hadn't thought about it like that.

"Poor people are just lazy and need to get a job," Anthony replied. "That's what my dad says."

Marisa jumped out of her chair. "Poor people aren't lazy. I know, because my family's been poor, and we've been hungry, too." Her face crumpled, then she fled the room.

Kara sat at her desk in shock. She'd never meant to hurt Marisa or anyone with this food drive. She put her head in her hands.

"What's the deal with this committee?" blustered Anthony. "At first I was sure it was a way for you and Nicole to stay after school and follow Mr. Gino, but Nicole didn't even join. And how was I supposed to know about Marisa being poor? Now I feel like a jerk."

Kara snapped, "How do you think she feels?"

Anthony's face flushed.

"I'm going to find Marisa." Kara stood up.

"I'll come, too," said Anthony.

They ran into the hall. Kara turned right—no one was there. She looked to her left: no Marisa.

Kara flew to the girls' rest room with Anthony behind her.

"You can't go in there!" Kara barked.

Anthony yelled, "Hey, Marisa, you in there?"

Kara stepped inside, slammed the door, and heaved herself against it. Anthony pounded, hollering, "I'm sorrrrry, Marisa! I didn't mean it."

Footsteps thundered down the hall, then Kara heard Mr. Gino's voice outside.

"Leave the girls alone," he told Anthony. More footsteps, followed by muffled protests. It sounded like Anthony was being dragged away.

Kara peered under the stalls. There, down at the end, were two skinny legs. Kara knocked on the door.

"Please come out, Marisa. I'm really sorry. You're right. We *should* help the poor."

Marisa unlocked the door and brushed past Kara. "Leave me alone. And don't feel sorry for me."

Kara flinched. "I don't feel sorry for you." But she did.

"We're not poor anymore," said Marisa. "But three years ago, my dad lost his job, and my mom was sick, so she couldn't work. We hardly had any money. I went with my mom to a food bank a few times, and they gave us groceries. At first I was embarrassed, but everybody was so nice. It made a big difference."

"So—do you still need food?" Kara asked gently.

"No. My dad's working again, and my mom's got a part-time job. We're doing fine." Marisa splashed her face in the sink, and Kara handed her a paper towel.

"I'm leaving," Marisa said. "You guys don't want me on the committee, so I quit."

"But I need you! With your help, this is going to be the best food drive ever!" said Kara.

Marisa brightened. "I know it can be! I wish we could do something fun, like have a contest."

"That's a great idea. We could give a prize to the class that donates the most food."

"But we don't have any money for a prize," said Marisa with a sigh.

"Then it has to be free," Kara said. The word "free" bounced in her mind like a pinball and turned into "freedom." That was it! She knew a great way to get kids to donate food, and it would get her into big trouble, too.

"I know!" Kara declared. "The grand prize is . . . a day off from school!"

"A day off from school! We can't do that. We'd need permission from Sister Mary Francis or Miss Monet."

"Naaah." Kara waved her hand. "They just left for a conference. Miss Monet said I was in charge, and Sister Mary Francis told me to get things off to a good start. You heard her say, 'Do whatever it takes'!"

"I'm not sure this is what she meant. We should ask someone, maybe the substitute teacher."

"Sure," said Kara. "Now let's work on the posters."

Glancing at her watch, Marisa said, "Mr. Gino's going to lock up soon. We could work at my house, though. I live right across the street."

Kara had hoped to get to Molly's house before dinner, but she couldn't say no to Marisa. Besides, she needed to create the right kind of posters—posters so outrageous that Sister Mary Francis would jump out of her skin when she saw them.

Chapter 14

A SIZZLING CAMPAIGN

Marisa lived across from the school in a big old house. The paint was peeling, and the chimney leaned over, but Kara liked the porch with its wide wicker swing, and the red welcome mat shaped like a tomato.

Marisa ran inside, calling, "I'm home, I'm home!"

Kara sniffed. Something smelled good. She trailed Marisa into the kitchen and saw an old lady pouring batter into a griddle. *Sizzle, crackle.* The woman lifted out something resembling a snow-flake and dropped it on a blue plate.

Marisa hugged the woman and spoke to her in Italian before turning to Kara. "This is Yummy," she said.

"What's yummy?"

"No, silly, this is my grandmother Yumzetti. We call her Yummy. She's visiting from Italy."

"Hi," Kara replied with a smile. Yummy patted Kara's head, prattling in Italian. She must have talked for five minutes.

"What's she saying?" Kara asked Marisa.

"She's happy that we're working on the food drive together. She likes it when kids do good things, and she wants to give you a present."

"A present? What for?"

Marisa shrugged. "Let's go see." The girls followed Marisa's grandmother into the dining room, where Yummy opened a hutch and lifted out a shiny wooden box with gold squiggles on it. Yummy sorted through a jumble of items—silver chains, little rocks, and rosary beads. Finally, she said "Ah!" and handed Kara a chain with an oval medal, which had an engraving of a girl riding a horse, and the words, *Jeanne d'Arc.*

As Yummy spoke, Marisa translated. "It's a Joan of Arc medal. She got it in France. She wants you to have it because you're working on the anniversary celebration."

"Oh, no! It's too valuable." Kara tried to hand it back, but Yummy slipped the medal over her neck. The cold chain made Kara's skin tingle.

"Don't worry. It's not worth a lot," said Marisa. "She bought it in a gift shop. Keep it, or you'll hurt her feelings."

"Thank you," said Kara. Yummy beamed.

"Come on, let's have a snack." Marisa pulled Kara into the kitchen and picked up the plate of snowflakes. "Try a *pizzelle*."

"Thanks." Kara bit into a wafer. It was sweet and delicious, as light as air.

The girls climbed a spiral staircase to an attic bedroom painted sky blue, with rainbows and stars stuck on the ceiling. Two sets of bunk beds lined the walls.

"Lucky for us, my sisters went to my cousin's house, so we have the place to ourselves." Marisa opened her closet and took out paper, poster board, and markers. The girls settled on the floor and doodled.

Feeling inspired, Kara wrote, *SISTER MARY FRANCIS SAYS: St. Joan of Arc wants you to give your food to the poor. If you don't, you'll go to the opposite place from heaven, where your buns will be toasted!*

Marisa giggled. " 'Buns will be toasted!' I love it!"

"Now for the artwork," said Kara. She used the bright yellow marker to draw two plump hot dog buns squeezed together, roasting over a fire.

Marisa studied the drawing. "Do you think it's too much?"

"We want to grab people's attention," Kara said. "We need to promote the contest, too. How about we add this: 'Don't be a fool, win a day off from school!'"

"Great!" Marisa said. The girls got busy making posters and a flier to send home to parents. When they finished, Marisa invited her to stay for dinner, and Kara realized her mother didn't even know where she was. She called home, expecting to be in trouble, but her mom told her to stay and have fun.

Dinner with the Yumzettis was noisy, with eight people gathered at the table, but Kara had a good time. She forgot about Molly until she got home and her mom said, "Molly called three times."

"Oh, no!" Kara ran upstairs and phoned her friend.

"What happened?" asked Molly. "I waited and waited for you."

"I'm really sorry, but I have a good reason." Kara spilled out the plans for the contest.

"A day off from school!" Molly whistled. "That's great. You'll get expelled for sure."

Kara couldn't resist saying, "Too bad Cheryl won't like it when I get back."

"Who cares?" Molly said airily. "I'm not talking to her anymore."

"You're not?" Kara sat down on her bed. "What happened?"

"Oh, we got into a fight. Cheryl wants us both to wear ponytails, and she wants me to wash my hair with horse shampoo. She uses it every day because she says it makes her hair shiny."

"Horse shampoo!" Kara giggled. "That girl's obsessed."

"Hey, did you make up with that friend of yours, the one looking for the body snatcher?" Molly asked.

"No, but I made a new friend named Marisa. She's really nice and cares about helping people. She'll do a great job with the food drive when I get kicked out."

"I can't wait till you get back. I really miss you."

"I miss you, too."

After the girls said good-bye, Kara grabbed her wall calendar and counted off days, writing *Freedom!* on the sixth day. That's when Sister Mary Francis would return and kick Kara out of school.

Chapter 15

A HABIT WITH AN ATTITUDE

Kara walked into class the next day, and her heart sank. The contest was dead for sure.

The substitute teacher was a nun, a very old nun. Her habit was so stiff, she must have sprayed it with a can of starch. Her wrinkled face had a million frown lines, and her black glasses looked like magnifying lenses.

Kara felt the nun's eyes upon her as she stashed the contest posters in her desk. She took her seat, clutching her Joan of Arc medal.

The nun rose and cleared her throat, sounding like a volcano about to explode. "I am Sister Blandina."

"Where'd they drag her from?" said Anthony, not bothering to whisper.

The nun's eyes blasted him. "I heard that. My hearing aid is a modern miracle. I'll tell you where I came from—the Mother House. You may think the Mother House is a rest home where old nuns go to die, but let me assure you, we are still kicking."

No one dared say a word.

Sister Blandina continued: "I'm delighted to spend a few days with you, but let me make one thing clear. I won't stand for nonsense." She pointed to a metal folding chair beside her desk. "If you fall from my graces, you will sit in the Fallen Angels chair."

Kara could see herself strapped there for days once Sister Blandina learned of her contest.

"Now let's get to work." Sister thumped over to the blackboard and pulled down a map. "Who can find Guatemala? I was a missionary there for thirty years."

After geography, Sister hosted a spelling bee, then led the class in jumping jacks, declaring, "Exercise clears the cobwebs from your brain!"

By lunchtime, Kara wanted to keel over, but she knew she had to face the nun.

She took a deep breath and approached Sister Blandina, with Marisa at her side. Kara spoke as fast as she could, telling Sister about the food drive, and how poor people needed their help. She breezed over the contest, making it sound like a done deal.

"I know about the food drive," Sister Blandina said. "Sister Mary Francis left a note asking me to look at the posters. Let me see them."

Kara shuffled to her desk, wishing she could crawl inside it. She brought a poster to Sister, who settled back in her chair and read aloud:

" 'Sister Mary Francis says: St. Joan of Arc wants you to give your food to the poor. If you don't, you'll go to the opposite place from heaven, where your buns will be toasted!' "

Sister Blandina studied the buns from different angles. Yesterday, those yellow buns had shined brilliantly. Now Kara knew she'd be the one roasting in the opposite place of heaven.

Sister read on: " 'Don't be a fool, win a day off from school!' Who came up with this?"

"I did." Kara knew what was coming next. Sister would declare that she was canceling the contest, confiscating the posters, and burning them in a bonfire at the Mother House.

"Very inventive," said Sister Blandina. "When I worked in the Guatemalan jungles, we had to do things creatively to get people's attention. I volunteer at the food bank, and I know supplies are low. Go forward and do God's work."

Kara could hardly believe her luck. She and Marisa took off, plastering posters all over school.

Before long, Kara felt like a rock star. Kids gave her high fives, and Colton Ryan, the cutest boy in the eighth grade, called out, "Yo, McKinney! Awesome contest!"

Kara puffed out. This day off from school was a great idea. Sister Mary Francis would still kick her out, but she couldn't revoke the holiday without a revolt. People would remember Kara McKinney, all right.

Only Anthony had nasty things to say. "I know what you're up to, Kara. You dreamed up this contest to keep the whole school busy while you snoop around after Mr. Gino. Well, I'm hot on this case, too, and I'll get my reward."

"You do that," said Kara. She'd be long gone before he cracked that case.

During recess the next day, Marisa went to the office to photocopy fliers, and Kara ducked into the rest room. She found Nicole looking out the window, binoculars pointed toward the woods.

"Hi," Kara said tentatively.

Nicole spun around and put down her binoculars. "Hello," she replied.

Both girls stared at the floor, until Kara finally said, "Nicole, I'm sorry about what I said."

"Me too." Relief flooded Nicole's face. "If you want to get kicked out, that's your choice. And it won't be long. Wait till Sister Mary Francis gets back!"

"Hello, Bingham, here I come," sang out Kara. "So anything new on Mr. Gino?"

"You bet. A reliable source told me he's taking the train into Philadelphia at night. He's moving into new areas, if you get my drift."

"Like other graveyards?" asked Kara.

"That's my theory. He's probably digging up bodies all over the city, but I still don't know his motive. You know, I could use more of your help on this case."

"I'll be gone soon, but we can snoop around some Saturday morning."

"Great. And if you need any help, just ask," Nicole said.

"Actually, I do. Could you help Marisa with the food drive after I leave?"

"Sure. I should have joined the committee to begin with." Nicole smiled, and Kara felt like somebody had snapped up the shades in a dark room, letting the sun pour in.

Chapter 16

THE SMOKING GUN

The contest took off like a horse race, with each class trying to nose its way ahead of the competition. The Friday before Sister Mary Francis's return, Kara asked Sister Blandina to unlock the principal's office, then she used a wagon to haul bags of donations to her office.

At recess, Kara called Marisa and Nicole together.

"Nicole, would you go look for Mr. Gino? We need boxes for food storage." Nicole sped off immediately. Kara asked Marisa to draw a big chart tracking each class's progress in the contest.

Meanwhile, Kara took charge of stacking cans and jars all over Sister's office.

She started with Sister Mary Francis's bookshelf, dusting off the top and piling it high with canned fruit. She created a pyramid of pineapples, pears, peaches, and prunes. She needed more room for fruit cocktail, by far the most popular donation, so she took books off the first shelf. Sister had a lot of religious books, but Kara was surprised to find scientific volumes on anatomy, botany, and physiology.

Next, Kara cleared the top of a filing cabinet, removing a picture of Sister visiting a shrine to St. Francis of Assisi. She loaded it with spaghetti sauce and pasta noodles in all shapes and sizes. She balanced Sister's picture atop a box of ziti noodles.

Whistling a happy tune, Kara filled a corner of the office with food she wasn't sure that people really ate. Sardines, anchovies, oyster soup, pickled pigs' feet, and other puzzling items. She heaped everything into towers, connecting them with bridges made out of cracker boxes.

As for Sister's desk, Kara chose just the right thing: fifteen cans of Joan of Arc brand black beans.

Kara stood back, admiring her work and imagining Sister Mary Francis's horror, when the school secretary barged in carrying a stack of folders.

"Kara McKinney, what in the world are you doing?" Mrs. Shuey demanded.

Kara gulped. "Oh, this is a surprise for Sister Mary Francis. She'll be so excited to see how much food we've collected!"

"No, she won't. This is a mess, and a safety hazard, too. Remove it at once."

"Please, I'll take it away after Sister gets back," Kara pleaded.

Mrs. Shuey slammed her folders on Sister's desk, knocking over several cans of Joan of Arc beans, which rolled around the room.

Behind her, Kara heard a volcano rumble. She swiveled to see Sister Blandina behind her, clearing her throat.

"Is there a problem?" asked Sister.

"Indeed there is," said Mrs. Shuey. "Kara won't listen. I want her to clear away this junk."

Sister Blandina sauntered around the room, her hands buried in her habit. She murmured, "My, oh my." As she headed for the bookcase, she tripped over a can of beans and tilted like a windmill, but recovered by grabbing a chair.

"Are you okay?" Kara asked, but she was thinking, Now I'm done for.

Sister gazed at Kara and said, "This packs a wallop. What a powerful impression. I like your fruit theme on the bookcase, and the Italian display on the filing cabinet. As for this sculpture"—Sister pointed to the towers—"it's a fine example of abstract art."

Kara wondered if Sister needed to go to the Mother House for a good, long rest.

Turning to Mrs. Shuey, Sister Blandina said, "I'm sorry Kara upset you with her enthusiasm. I'm sure she wants to give Sister Mary Francis a welcome-back surprise."

"That's it exactly!" Kara said.

"And our food drive is going very well," Sister reported. "The Harvest Food Bank is so grateful to be chosen for our project. Did you know they serve fifty thousand meals every year, right here in our community?"

"Wow, I'm glad we can help," said Kara, feeling a flash of pride.

"That is admirable," said Mrs. Shuey.

Sister Blandina went on, "Now, Kara, clear the cans off Sister's desk. You can leave the rest of the display here for one day, then take it to the basement."

"I suppose that's all right," said Mrs. Shuey, and she left with Sister Blandina.

Kara heaved a sigh of relief. As she cleared the desk, she caught sight of a paper in Sister Mary Francis's in-box that had Mr. Gino's name typed on it. It was a printout of an e-mail.

Her heart beating fast, Kara scanned the text.

Gino—I trust things are moving along on our project. Remember to maintain the utmost secrecy. I've talked discreetly to sources in Florida, and I'm sure our experiments will prove interesting to others beyond our local area. This could be bigger than we ever dreamed. Sister Mary Francis.

Gino had scrawled a reply at the bottom. *Dear Sister, no point e-mailing back, because you've checked out of the hotel. I agree that others will one day view our experiments as "groundbreaking." Everything is moving along, but we have too many dead ones back there. I'll work more at night. Some kids have been nosing around.*

The smoking gun! Kara dropped the e-mail on the desk and collapsed in a chair. This body snatching was bigger than Mr. Gino. Sister was in on it too, and possibly others. Kara wondered what hideous experiments they were conducting, and why.

Chapter 17

CONSPIRACY THEORIES

Back in the classroom, Kara passed Nicole a note: *Urgent. Meet me in Sister Mary Francis's office after school. I'll show you something that will blow this case wide open!*

The minute the final bell rang, Nicole and Kara dashed to the office. Marisa followed them.

"Hi, Marisa," Kara said. "Nicole's going to help me finish the food display. You've done so much work, you deserve a break."

"Break? Are you kidding? I have to go grocery shopping with Yummy. If I don't watch her, she gets carried away with buy-one-get-one-free sales. But I can stay a minute. I want to see all the food."

No sooner had the girls entered Sister's office than Anthony intruded.

"I'm on the committee too," he said. "Give me some food to count!"

Kara gritted her teeth. "Thanks, but Nicole's helping us."

Anthony lunged for a bag Kara had left in a corner. "I'll take that!"

"Back off, you lunatic!" said Nicole.

"You can't keep me off this committee," roared Anthony.

Sister Blandina marched in. "Anthony Russo, come with me! Trouble seems to follow you wherever you go. I'd hate to have to mention this to your great-aunt, Sister Bernadette. She lives with me at the Mother House, and just the other day, she was saying that she wished you'd come visit her."

"I can't do that," Anthony said. "Every time my parents come back from a visit, I hear about weird stuff going on there."

"Interesting," said Sister Blandina. As she carted him away, Anthony called back, "I'm still on the committee, no matter what!"

"That kid has a problem with authority figures," said Nicole.

"You know what I think?" said Marisa. "I think he wants to be on our committee because he's lonely. I don't see him hanging out with other kids."

"That's because he repels them with deviant actions," declared Nicole.

"Yeah, he spit on me on the first day of school," said Kara.

"Maybe he just wants attention." Marisa gazed around the room and whistled. "Wow, look at all this food! Just think how many families we can help. I can't wait to tell Yummy." She left to go home.

Kara tiptoed across the hall to the main office. Mrs. Shuey was putting on her jacket. She told Kara, "I have to leave early. You girls finish up and go straight home."

As soon as Mrs. Shuey disappeared, Kara ran back to Sister's office and grabbed the e-mail. "Check this out."

Nicole's face paled as she read it. "It's a criminal conspiracy! Mr. Gino has manipulated Sister Mary Francis into assisting with his crimes. He must know something about her and threatened to expose her if she didn't cooperate."

"Blackmail?" Kara said.

"Could be. Or here's another theory—Sister's the mastermind, and Mr. Gino is her puppet."

"Let me show you something else." Kara led Nicole to the pile of the books she'd pulled from Sister's shelf. "Look at these science books on anatomy and stuff."

"Anatomy, that's the study of bodies," Nicole exclaimed. "So Sister is reading about dissecting bodies."

"But why? What kind of experiments could they be doing?"

"Let me think." Nicole sat down, her brow furrowed. "I read a case study once about a criminal ring that was selling corpses to unethical scientists."

"Maybe that was a horror movie you watched," Kara said.

"No, I swear, I read it in a textbook. These crazy scientists believed they could bring the dead back to life. They were willing to pay big money to suppliers of cadavers. And when it comes to crime, greed is a primary motivator."

"Sister and Mr. Gino would have to be desperate to do something like that."

"Let's think why they'd need money," Nicole mused.

Kara settled on a crate of juice bottles and pondered. "Well, Mr. Gino is an immigrant. Maybe he has to send money home to his family."

"I think he's an orphan," Nicole said. "But being an immigrant can be a hard-knock life. Maybe he doesn't want to wait twenty years to save money for a house or a business. That would explain his need. But what about Sister Mary Francis?"

As Kara mulled over the question, her eyes landed on the picture of Sister at the shrine of St. Francis of Assisi.

"Wait! Sister told me she loves visiting shrines and wants to tour them all, but she doesn't have the time or money to do it."

"There's your motive!" said Nicole. "And her fascination with shrines throws a new light on things. Some people believe miracles happen there. Here's a possibility: Sister made a pilgrimage to a shrine and discovered a miraculous formula. Like making body parts grow again. She and Mr. Gino are experimenting with it. With that kind of information, they could be rich."

"This is too much for me," said Kara. "Boy, am I glad I'm getting out of here. I think we should go to the police."

"Are you kidding? They'll take the case away from us. I need to make a copy of this smoking gun." Nicole took the e-mail and zipped into Mrs. Shuey's office.

Kara went home smiling. She'd helped Nicole by finding an important clue. And in just a few days, she'd be kicked out of school.

Chapter 18

THROWN OFF COURSE

On Monday, Kara hurried into class. She watched the clock, and a terrible hour passed. Finally, Sister's voice boomed over the public-address system: "Kara McKinney, report to the office at once!"

Kara jumped up and winked at Nicole. This was it, her last day.

Sister Mary Francis shook a poster at Kara, barking, "A day off from school? Who gave you permission?"

"No one. You weren't here, so I decided, Go for it!"

Sister waved her arms. "Look at this mess! A pickle jar toppled over, and I had to mop pickle juice off my floor."

"I'm sorry," Kara said.

Her eyes narrowing, Sister commanded, "Sit down, young lady."

Kara settled on a hard wooden chair. The nun picked up a pen and began writing on a yellow tablet, her fingers forming a strong fist.

The hand of God, thought Kara. Strike me down and banish me.

Sister Mary Francis opened a bulging file. Kara smiled. It was probably the paperwork for her dismissal.

"Archbishop Ryan called this morning to inquire about this contest," said Sister.

Kara sat up straight. News sure traveled fast to the top banana. Archbishop Ryan was head of all the Catholic dioceses in the Philadelphia area.

"He wanted to know all about this contest, a contest I did not authorize."

"Oh, boy! I bet he's mad," Kara said.

Sister tapped her fingers on her desk. "Mad? That's not the word I'd use."

"Furious, then? He must want me expelled."

"Not exactly," Sister said. "You see, his nephew Colton is in eighth grade here, and Colton told him all about the contest. The archbishop thinks it's brilliant that we're inspiring hundreds of children to think of the poor. And I wasn't about to contradict him, not when I'm trying to get five thousand dollars from him for a new roof."

"Huh?"

"What I'm saying, Kara, is that the contest will go on. But you're not off the hook." Sister shook a finger at her. "Young lady, you are an unguided missile."

Kara rose. "Well, you won't want me around anymore. I'm dangerous. And unpredictable."

"Is that so?" Sister arched an eyebrow. "I think I know why you cooked up this contest, and you'll see it through."

"But, Sister, I didn't even ask your permission."

The nun's lips twitched. "Some would say, Better to ask for forgiveness than permission."

Stunned, Kara sank down in her chair.

Sister Mary Francis went on, "Yes, my dear, you are an unguided missile, but I will keep you on course. You have great potential. Sister Blandina thinks so, too."

"Sister Blandina?"

"She left a note recommending that I send you to a youth leadership workshop in Philadelphia in November. It's a weekend retreat, and Sister Blandina is in charge."

Kara's blood ran cold. Maybe they were trying to turn her into a nun!

"Sister Blandina left you a gift, too," said the principal, passing Kara a book.

Kara stared at the cover picture. It was Sister Blandina, swinging a machete through jungle brush. She wore khakis, a safari shirt, and a crucifix around her neck. The book was titled *My Spiritual Journey in the Guatemalan Jungles*.

Opening the book, Kara read the inscription: *To Kara. Remember that Christ broke the rules, too, but always for the right reasons. Sister Blandina.*

"I can't go to her retreat," Kara blurted out. "I'm busy every weekend."

"I'll talk to your parents about it. I'm sure they'll be excited about the opportunity." Sister gave Kara a steely smile.

Sighing, Kara got up to go.

"Not yet, Kara. I have one other item to discuss. It's about our anniversary celebration next week. I'd like you to give a speech about the food drive, thanking everyone for their support."

A speech. No way. Her parents would love it, and Kara would be stuck here forever.

"I can't do it," Kara said. "I've got terrible stage fright."

"Funny, I've heard you love to perform." Sister put away Kara's file. "Now why don't you head back to class? You've got plenty to think about."

Kara was so depressed, she couldn't talk to Nicole or Marisa for the rest of the day. When school ended, she tried to slip out the door, but Sister Mary Francis nabbed her.

"Would you drop off this letter at the rectory for me, Kara? Father DiMarini needs this report right away, and I have a million things to do."

So I'm her little nun-in-training, off to do her errands, thought Kara.

She took the letter and collapsed on a bench outside the school. A sigh escaped from the depths of her soul. Instead of disgracing herself, she'd been recruited for the nunnery.

Sister Kara. Just the thought gave her shivers.

"Why me?" Kara buried her head in her hands. "Why me?"

Chapter 19

DEADLY DISCOVERIES

A light rain began to fall as Kara trudged over to the rectory. Ivy vines covered the gray stone building, which stood in the church's shadow. She took the stairs two at a time, shoved the letter into the mail slot, and charged back down the mossy steps. Kara skidded, tumbling over a low wall and landing in a clump of prickly bushes.

"Ouch!" Kara rubbed her arm and picked up her backpack. Pens and pencils rolled all over the ground. Great, she'd torn the lining.

Not far away, a door slammed. Kara saw Mr. Gino leaving the church basement, carrying a stack of books and papers. A man in a black leather jacket followed him.

"Gino, you've got to stop," the man said. "You're becoming obsessed."

Kara ducked down.

"I can't stop now," Mr. Gino said. "I'm almost out of time."

"What's taking so long?"

"Try digging six feet under at midnight and see how fast you work," Mr. Gino snapped.

Icy fingers of fear crawled up Kara's spine.

The man in the black jacket said, "I thought when I made those deliveries for you last week, that was it."

"All I need is another few days." Mr. Gino stopped near the shrubs where Kara cowered. "Can you come back tonight to help me? About midnight?"

"No, I can't risk it. I've done my part." The man stalked into the parking lot and pulled away in a long black car. Kara's eyes bugged. A hearse! The man's "deliveries" must have been coffins.

Mr. Gino watched the hearse drive off, and muttered in Italian. From his tone, Kara was sure he'd cursed. He shifted his books, which were stacked so high they hit his nose, and hurried down the sidewalk.

Suddenly pens and pencils rolled under his shoes and he crashed to the ground, books and papers flying everywhere. He landed inches from Kara. His bloodshot eyes locked with hers, and Kara stifled a scream.

Mr. Gino leaped up. "What are you doing there?"

"I dropped something." Kara's heart began thumping. "What are you doing?"

"Going to the library." Mr. Gino scrambled to pick up the mess.

Kara grabbed several books, glancing at the titles: *Cemeteries Around the World, Monuments to the Dead,* and *From Dead Limbs to Life.*

"I'll take those," said Mr. Gino. As he snatched them, Kara nabbed a piece of paper blowing by. It was a hand-drawn map of the school, cemetery, and woods. Someone had scribbled Italian words all over it and had marked *X*s in certain spots.

"What's this?" Kara asked.

Mr. Gino seized the map, warning Kara: "Don't tell anyone about this." Then he rushed into the parking lot and drove off in an old blue pickup. Its muffler rumbled, and a dark plume of smoke snaked around. It formed the shape of the letter *T.*

T for *Trouble.* Well, she'd had enough trouble for today.

* * *

Kara raced home and went straight to her room. Her mother came in and handed her the phone. "It's Nicole."

Kara waited until her mother left. "Hello?" she breathed.

"Are you okay? What happened with Sister Mary Francis?"

Kara spilled out everything—her talk with Sister, her encounter with Mr. Gino, her fear that she might be a nun in the making.

"Calm down, Kara. It's all becoming clear to me. I think you were sent to our school for a reason."

"Like what?"

"To help me expose this criminal ring: Mr. Gino, Sister Mary Francis, and the guy with the hearse. And if we can prove they're experimenting on dead bodies, think of the scandal! Your parents will pull you out of school so fast, your head will spin."

"They won't believe me," said Kara. She flopped on her bed.

"They will if we have evidence. Let's investigate the woods."

The last thing Kara needed was a grave-digging expedition. "My parents won't let me."

"Detectives don't ask their parents for permission," said Nicole scornfully. There was a long silence, and Kara could almost hear the wheels turning in her friend's mind.

"I've got another great idea," Nicole said. "Sister Mary Francis wants you to give a speech. You can say a few words about the food drive, then whammy—tell everyone about the body-snatching ring! TV stations will be there, and they'll go crazy over the story."

"You're nuts!"

"Think about it, Kara. Won't Molly die when she sees your face all over TV!"

Kara pictured herself on stage, facing a huge crowd. She saw lights flashing, cameras rolling, and reporters dangling microphones in her face. Molly sure would be impressed to see Kara on the news. And Kara's parents would be horrified to learn about Mr. Gino and Sister.

"You have to do it," said Nicole. "Otherwise, Sister Blandina will be measuring you for a nun's habit."

Kara shuddered. "Let me think about this. I'll call you back." Immediately Kara phoned Molly, and for once, her friend answered.

"Hi, Kara. Can you hold a sec? I'm on the phone with Cheryl."

Kara protested, "I thought you weren't talking to her anymore."

"Oh, we made up. I'll be right back." With a click, Molly put Kara on hold.

Kara felt her cheeks flush, and she clenched her teeth in frustration.

When Molly came back on the line, she sounded breathless. "So did you get kicked out today? Tell me yes!"

"Not exactly," Kara stammered. "I still need a little more time."

"That's too bad. But we could get together this weekend. Cheryl and I are in a horse show Saturday. Do you want to come?"

"No, thanks."

"Come on, we never do anything fun together." Molly's voice hung heavy with disappointment.

"You're the one who's always too busy for me."

"I am not! I just invited you to my show. So what if Cheryl's there? We can't do everything by ourselves all the time."

"I'm busy with a secret mission," Kara said. "I don't have time for a horse show. Good-bye." She hung up and called Nicole back.

"Okay, I'm with you," Kara told her.

"Great," Nicole said. "Tomorrow, I'll show you my notebook outlining my theories. It'll blow your mind."

Chapter 20

THE BODY DETECTIVES

The next day before classes, Nicole pulled Kara aside and opened her red notebook, but Anthony strutted over and she had to slam it shut.

"Having a secret meeting about the food drive?" he said. "What's going on with the contest anyway?"

"The third grade's ahead by fourteen cans of spaghetti sauce," replied Kara.

"The little creeps," Anthony muttered.

Kara made a sudden decision. "Anthony, a bunch of food came in yesterday, and it's in the basement. Maybe somebody donated candy bars. You could count the food during recess, if you want."

"Are you going to help?" he asked.

"I'd like to, but Nicole and I have to work on a speech." Kara smiled at him. "We could really use your help."

After lunch, Anthony scurried off while Kara stayed in the classroom with Marisa and Nicole. Miss Monet had recess duty, so the girls were alone.

"Hey, Marisa, do you live across from the school?" Nicole asked.

"Yeah." Marisa was filling in a chart tracking the food drive progress.

"Good," Nicole said. "You can keep an eye on Mr. Gino after hours."

"What?" exclaimed Kara.

"We need all the help we can get," said Nicole. "It's time we told her."

"You never said you were dragging Marisa into this."

"What's the big secret?" said Marisa, putting down her gel pen.

Nicole pulled Marisa so close their noses touched. "You can't tell anyone, but Mr. Gino is digging up bodies in the graveyard and storing them in the woods. He and Sister Mary Francis are conducting experiments on cadavers. If they succeed, they can make big money."

Marisa exploded with laughter. "Why would Sister Mary Francis need money? Nuns take a vow of poverty."

"She has dreams of traveling the world to visit shrines," said Nicole. "That costs big bucks."

Kara remembered something. "And she needs five thousand dollars to fix the school roof."

Nicole went on to tell Marisa about the hole that Mr. Gino had dug in the graveyard and the late-night deliveries with the hearse.

Marisa's eyes widened. "This is so weird. Last week I saw lights in the woods late at night. I sleep in the attic, so I can see the school and the woods." Then she shook her head. "But that doesn't prove anything. And there's no way Sister's involved in anything criminal."

"Look at this." Nicole whipped out her note-book, flipping to a page. "Read this e-mail from Sister Mary Francis."

As Marisa read it, her fingers began to tremble.

"You see, we aren't crazy," Nicole said. "And it's not just our graveyard they're after. One of my sources spotted Mr. Gino in the cemetery near St. Joseph's University."

"What source?" asked Kara.

"My sister Jeannine."

"Your sister?" Kara had expected Nicole to have a mysterious source, a shady man with a name like Dirtbag. The kind you saw on TV detective shows.

"Yeah, she goes to college at St. Joe's, and she's seen Mr. Gino lurking around campus. I begged her to follow him, and she finally agreed to do it because she thinks he's cute." Nicole snorted. "So she tailed him one night and found him in the cemetery, but she freaked out and fled the scene."

"Scary," breathed Marisa. "Someone should call the police."

"The cops won't listen to us," said Nicole. "They want evidence, and not just e-mails. That's why we have to stake out the woods."

A shadow fell across the room, and Sister Mary Francis loomed in the doorway. "Hello, girls."

All three girls froze.

"How's the contest coming along?" Sister asked.

Kara recovered first. "Great!" she trilled. "Only three more days to go."

"Keep up the good work," said Sister as she left.

Kara peered outside to make sure she was gone. "Whew, that was close. Look, we need a plan. The anniversary celebration is just a week away. Why don't you guys spend the night at my house Friday, and we'll think up something?"

"Sounds good," Nicole said. "Marisa, you in?"

Marisa shuffled her feet and didn't answer.

"Do you want criminals at our school?" pressed Nicole.

"No," Marisa said. "My sisters go here. I don't want them in danger, or anybody else, either."

"So we're all in this together?" asked Kara.

Marisa and Nicole nodded.

"Friday it is then," cried Kara. The girls clasped hands, and a thrill of excitement coursed through Kara.

Chapter 21

TROUBLE COMES IN THREES

Kara almost didn't make it until Friday. She'd heard trouble came in threes, and that's exactly what happened.

First, the food drive heated up. Every class wanted to win that day off from school, and some kids would stop at nothing to win.

On Wednesday, as students lined up to go into school, a white pickup truck pulled into the parking lot. The truck was full of cages, and Kara heard squawking.

A man called out, "Delivery for Sister Mary Francis."

Sister was inside the building, so Miss Monet walked over to the man. Kara watched in surprise as a second-grader named Angie scooted to the truck and climbed in the back.

"Hooray, they're all here!" Angie yelled.

Suddenly dozens of turkeys hopped out and raced around the playground. Kids went crazy chasing the birds. Turkey feathers flew everywhere. One turkey pooped on Claire Daniels's foot, and she started crying hysterically.

Sister Mary Francis stormed outside. "What is the meaning of this?"

A girl shouted, "Ask Angie Boyd!"

Kara hurried over to Angie as Sister approached.

Twisting her curls, Angie explained, "These turkeys are for the food drive. They came from my uncle's farm. Each bird feeds fifteen people, and we have thirty turkeys. We should get credit for feeding four hundred and fifty people."

"We're not accepting live donations," said Sister. "Take them back to the farm."

Mr. Gino arrived on the scene, and with the help of some boys, he herded the birds into the truck. Kara plucked a turkey feather off her shoe and sighed. How did things ever get this crazy?

Kara's second trouble came from Nicole. That week, Nicole ranted about criminal theories and carried her notebook everywhere, recording ideas to catch Mr. Gino. Once she almost left her notebook in the girls' rest room; luckily, Kara was with her and rescued it.

"Let me see this," Kara said.

The notebook was divided into sections: Mr. Gino; Sister Mary Francis; Conspiracy Theories; and Plans to Bust the Ring.

Kara flipped to the Mr. Gino section and read:

Hypothesis: Mr. Gino won't reveal his full name or hometown because he's on the lam. An Internet search of the world's most wanted criminals revealed a picture resembling Mr. Gino (he must have shaved his beard). The bounty for his head: $500,000.

Physical description: In the past month, his muscles have grown bigger. Otherwise, he has deteriorated. He is pale, and his eyes are bleary. His fingernails are dirty, his hands rough and red. He has started wearing heavy cologne to cover up the stench of bodies.

Incriminating statements: I heard Mrs. Wheeler, the sixth grade teacher, ask Mr. Gino what he'd been up to lately. He cackled and replied, "Conducting experiments."

Motivations for crime: Greed, delusions of power, pathological interest in corpses.

Summary: Mr. Gino and Sister Mary Francis are kingpins in a criminal ring. They are working with Ghoul Man, who drives a hearse. Sister made contacts in Florida to sell their experimental research and to ship bodies to. Miss Monet traveled with her and can't be ruled out as a suspect. Nor can Father DiMarini, who warned kids to stay out of the graveyard.

Kara shut the notebook. "That's good. Bring it to the slumber party."

"Wait till you see the plan I have to catch Mr. Gino," Nicole replied.

By Friday, Nicole was so excited about the sleepover, she babbled to herself during class and got detention for disturbing everyone. After school, Nicole skulked to the office, and Kara and Marisa trooped down to the basement to count food. It was the last day for the contest.

Sister Mary Francis stopped them. "I'll finish this over the weekend. That way the winner will be a surprise."

Kara figured Sister wanted to make sure no one had smuggled in more animals. She was glad to go home to get ready for the party. That's when the third bad thing happened.

The doorbell rang at six o'clock, thirty minutes early. Kara opened the front door to find Nicole on the doorstep, her red hair a wild mess, and her face drained of color. She burst out, "Kara, my notebook's gone! Someone stole it!"

Chapter 22

OPERATION CCG

"Stolen?" Kara cried. "Let's go to my bedroom, so my mom can't hear." The girls ran upstairs and shut the door.

Nicole said, "I thought I had it with me in detention, but when I checked my backpack, it wasn't there. So I ran back to the classroom, and guess who I found? Mr. Gino! He was emptying the trash, and he gave me a funny look. As soon as he left, I searched my desk, but my notebook was gone. I know he took it!"

"Did you write about our sleepover?" Kara asked.

Nicole nodded miserably. "What if he shows up here to stop us?"

"Don't be silly. He won't," said Kara, but the hairs on her neck prickled.

Outside, a truck pulled up. Kara saw Marisa climb out, dragging her sleeping bag. Kara and Nicole clumped downstairs, and Kara took her friends into the kitchen.

"It's so nice to meet you girls," said Kara's mother warmly.

Nicole piped up, "Mrs. McKinney, do you have a burglar alarm?"

"No, but don't worry, honey. This is a safe neighborhood."

Kara said quickly, "Do you have snacks for us, Mom?"

"Sure. So what's the plan tonight? A movie?"

"Maybe later. First we have to do a little work on the food drive."

"You girls sure have worked hard. I'm proud of you." Kara's mother loaded them with popcorn, cheese crackers, and sodas, and the girls went into the family room.

Nicole walked over to Kara's dog, Malabar, who was sleeping by the fireplace. She crouched down to inspect the black Lab's big ears.

"What are you doing?" asked Kara.

"Checking for bugs." Nicole patted down his fur.

"He doesn't have bugs!" Kara said.

"Not insects. The kind of bug that Mr. Gino would plant to monitor our activities."

Marisa reached for popcorn and laughed. "Nicole, don't you think you're going a little overboard?"

Nicole scrambled to her feet. "Well, the dog's clean."

Kara said, "Now let's get to work. After all, we have a grave robber to catch. That's what Operation CCG is all about."

"CCG?" said Marisa.

"Crusade to Catch Gino," said Kara proudly. "We need a code word for our mission."

Nicole smiled. "I like how your mind works, McKinney." She yanked papers from her backpack and spread them across the carpet. "Let's huddle. I made a map of the woods so we can locate the bodies."

"Wow, look at this." Kara traced a line marked *Trail to Dead Bodies*.

"We can't go through here," said Marisa, pointing to a section on the map. "That's not a trail, that's a ditch."

"Hmm," said Nicole. "I couldn't go back there, so I used an old map from the library. Are you sure?"

"Positive. When we moved in, I went exploring with my sister. In fact, we saw Mr. Gino digging that ditch. We played in there after he left."

"Marisa!" Nicole threw down her red pencil. "You may have trampled important evidence."

"We didn't go back again. We tracked home so much mud, my mom wouldn't let us play in the woods anymore."

Nicole marked *Mr. Gino's Victims* on her map. "Now we know where the bodies are, so let's talk about supplies for the raid. Kara, did you make a list?"

"You bet." Kara pulled a paper from her pocket. "First item, walkie-talkies. In case we get separated in the woods."

"Or captured by Mr. Gino," said Nicole.

"Captured?" Marisa squeaked.

"She's only kidding," said Kara. "I'll bring the walkie-talkies. Let's see, we need binoculars."

"I'll bring those," Marisa said. "My grandmother has a pair for bird watching."

"Don't bother," said Nicole. "I've got the kind with night vision."

"It won't be nighttime," Marisa said.

"I know, but these binoculars are incredibly powerful," retorted Nicole.

Kara interrupted, "You can both bring them. The

more binoculars, the better. Let's see, we need a camera, the kind that develops pictures right away."

"Yummy just bought a digital camera to e-mail her friends in Italy. I think she'll let me use it, since it's for a school project."

"Great." Kara scanned her list. "Last item: a cell phone, in case we need to call the police."

"I'll bring one," said Nicole. "Now let's go over the plan to catch Mr. Gino. On Monday, we'll scout the woods, locate the bodies, and take pictures of the evidence."

"What if Mr. Gino's back there?" asked Marisa.

"He won't be," Nicole said. "He has to get the school cleaned up for the anniversary celebration. The next day, Kara and I will make the announcement during her speech."

"I thought Kara was giving a speech about the food drive!" Marisa said. She put down her soda, looking upset.

"I am," said Kara. "The food drive is really important, but we have to let people know what Sister and Mr. Gino are up to, before it's too late."

"We'll ruin the event!" protested Marisa. "Let's pick another time."

"No, we want the live press coverage," Nicole insisted.

Kara saw Marisa's troubled face and deliberated. "I have an idea. We'll do interviews about the food drive, too. I'll put together a list of food banks, and we can hand that out. That way people will know how to keep helping the poor."

Marisa agreed, and Kara decided they needed a break. She popped in a movie, *Arachnophobia,* about killer spiders invading a town. Soon the girls were clutching one another, laughing and screaming.

After the movie, Kara's mother came in. "Girls, it's ten-thirty. Lights out in five minutes." Mrs. McKinney slid the dead bolt on the glass door leading to the deck.

Kara spread out her sleeping bag and was drifting off to sleep when Nicole whispered, "Did you hear that? Someone's knocking on that sliding door."

Kara sat up. She could make out shadows on the wall; they looked like trees blowing in the wind. "It's probably a branch hitting the window."

"No, I heard a knock," Nicole said, her voice quivering. "There it is again."

Sighing, Kara said, "I'll check the lock."

A beam of light moved across the glass door. The light flickered, then went out.

"It's Mr. Gino!" shrieked Nicole. "He's come for us!"

"Help! Help!" the girls cried.

Amid the panic, Kara heard heavy steps on the stairs. Her father rushed in, snapping on the light. "What's wrong?"

Kara threw her arms around him. "Dad, there's someone on the deck. We saw a flashlight!"

"Calm down. I'll check it out." Her father strode across the room and opened the door. A blast of cold air rushed in, making Kara's flannel gown billow. Malabar settled at Kara's feet.

Outside, Kara heard a noise, like someone coughing.

"Sic 'em, Malabar!" said Kara, but the dog whimpered and didn't move.

Mr. McKinney shut the door. "Just to be safe, I'll call the police."

Within minutes, a patrol car pulled into the driveway. An officer came up the sidewalk, swooshing his flashlight. Kara's father explained the situation.

"I'm Officer Clark. I'll take care of this." He was a stocky man with a bandage over his big red nose. Maybe a criminal punched him. Kara noticed a gun on his hip and swallowed. She hoped he wasn't going to have to shoot someone, here at her house.

As Officer Clark vanished into the shadows, the girls scrambled back to the family room. Mr. Mc-

Kinney flipped on the outdoor light, and cracked the door open to hear what was going on.

A pale moon hung in the sky, casting a ghostly light on the backyard. The officer prowled around, his feet crunching leaves and twigs. His flashlight made orange-yellow circles on the shrubs. When he kicked a bush, someone groaned.

Officer Clark jerked a body from a holly bush and ripped off a ski mask.

"Do you know this person?" he demanded.

Nicole screamed.

"Oh, no!" said Kara. "It can't be!"

Chapter 23

THE PROWLER

Officer Clark dragged the prowler inside. "What is your name?" he demanded.

"Harry Potter," said the burglar sullenly.

"He's not Harry Potter!" Kara said. "He's Anthony Russo. A kid in my class."

Kara couldn't believe Anthony was standing in her family room. His black jeans were covered with dirt, twigs stuck out of his hair, and he had a mud-splattered backpack draped over his shoulder.

The officer said, "Why are you trying to scare these girls?"

Anthony's eyes dropped to the floor, and his Adam's apple wobbled.

"What on earth is going on?" Kara's mother hurried into the room, her eyes wide with alarm.

"I'm no burglar," blustered Anthony. "Um, I was just checking up on the food drive. They keep having secret meetings, trying to leave me out."

"A likely story," snorted Nicole.

"You think you're so smart, Nicole," Anthony said. "I know you're trying to cut me out of the reward. So there's a five hundred thousand dollar bounty, huh?"

"I don't know what you're talking about," Nicole said coldly. "Officer, I think you should search him."

"Let's take a look in your backpack," said Officer Clark.

Grumbling, Anthony pulled out a Hershey bar, a flashlight, and a red notebook.

"My notebook!" Nicole seized it. "You are a recalcitrant deviant."

"What's that, little lady?" asked the policeman.

"A recalcitrant deviant is someone who goes out of his way to be a jerk," said Nicole with a satisfied smile.

"He's no deviant," said Officer Clark. "I see these kinds of pranks all the time. Come on, Anthony, I'm taking you home." Without warning, Anthony yanked open the door and took off like a jackrabbit into the night.

"Get back here!" Officer Clark pounded after him. Everybody dashed onto the deck, jostling for the best view. Kara watched the policeman chase Anthony around and around a birch tree. She felt a cold nose on her toes, then Malabar streaked by. With a not-so-ferocious bark, the dog leaped on Anthony and knocked him flat on his back. Anthony tried to get up, but Malabar hopped onto his chest and began chewing his shoe.

"Get this slobbering beast off me!" yelled Anthony, flailing his arms and legs like an upside-down bug.

"Not such a tough guy now, are you?" Officer Clark helped Anthony up and hauled him to the squad car, which disappeared into the night.

Kara's mother said, "Okay, everyone back to bed before we wake up the whole neighborhood."

The girls crawled into their sleeping bags and waited until Kara's parents trooped upstairs, then they began laughing hysterically. Within moments, Kara's father reappeared and said, "I'm not leaving until you go to sleep."

The next day, after Nicole and Marisa left, Kara hustled upstairs to call Molly about the sleepover. Suddenly she remembered the fight they'd had.

This stinks, Kara thought. I can't even tell my best friend about the most exciting night of my life.

She thought about their argument. Maybe she had wigged out.

She went to the computer in the family room and sent Molly an e-mail apologizing for being rude and wishing her good luck at the horse show.

Then Kara got busy doing research. She went on-line and found locations for food banks all over Philadelphia and statistics on hunger. Writing the speech was cool, because she had something important to say.

Now there was only one thing left to do: catch Mr. Gino.

Chapter 24

FOILED

On Monday, Kara was primed to launch Operation CCG—Crusade to Catch Gino. She met up with Nicole and Marisa on the playground at lunchtime recess.

"Remember, all we have to do today is locate the bodies and take pictures," said Nicole.

Suddenly a crowd of kids rushed up. "Hey, Kara, tell us about Anthony getting captured by the police," Claire Daniels said.

"How'd you know?" Kara asked.

"Nicole told me."

A guilty look crossed Nicole's face. "I had to tell someone. If I keep my emotions bottled up, I could develop post-traumatic stress disorder."

"You must have been so scared, Kara," said Monica Nunziata.

"Not really. My killer dog, Malabar, protected me. He's the one that captured Anthony."

A murmur of approval rippled through the crowd. Kara basked in the attention. Nicole and Marisa stood by her, nodding and smiling.

Anthony strutted over. "That's not true. That dog was a wimp, and the policeman didn't even handcuff me."

"You're a thief," Nicole said. "You stole my notebook."

"Yeah, because you keep cutting me out of the action. How else am I supposed to find out what's going on?"

"This is a girls' case, not a boys'," retorted Nicole.

"Oh, yeah? Don't forget I'm the one who pointed you to Mr. Gino."

Kara wanted to settle things down. "That's right, you did, and we appreciate it, Anthony."

"What are you guys talking about?" Claire asked.

"The food drive," said Kara. "It's a complicated story."

Anthony glared at Nicole. "I think I'll tell Sister Mary Francis about this and spoil your fun."

Just then, Sister Mary Francis strode over, blowing her whistle. "Break it up. Anthony, go inside right now."

As Anthony slunk off, kids scattered like dandelions in the breeze. Kara tried to dart away, but Sister caught her arm. "I'd like a word with you. Alone. Have you written your speech for tomorrow?"

"Yes, Sister. I'm all set."

"Good. I'd like you and your committee onstage, along with our honored guests. After you finish your remarks, I'll announce the contest winner."

"Oh, tell me now!"

"You'll have to wait," replied Sister. "By the way, Sister Blandina called and you're approved for the leadership workshop."

"Great," Kara murmured.

"Not only that, but she has an extra spot, so I can send someone else."

"That's good news," said Kara, knowing she'd be gone by then.

Sister went inside just as the bell sounded. Marisa and Nicole hurried over, their faces anxious.

"We missed our chance!" said Nicole. "We'll have to abandon the scouting mission."

"It's a bad omen," said Marisa. "We'd better call this off."

"No way," declared Nicole. "We can get everything done at recess tomorrow, and we'll still have time to make our announcement. Right, Kara?"

"You bet." Kara tried to sound confident, but a worm of worry gnawed at her.

That night, her worry grew from the size of an inchworm to a tapeworm. She wanted to talk to Molly, and sending an e-mail apology hadn't been good enough, so Kara called her to say she was sorry.

"That's okay." Molly took a deep breath. "Sometimes I get jealous of your new friends, too."

"You do?"

"Yeah. But we're in different schools, and things change. It would be boring if everything always stayed the same. But we're still friends, no matter what."

"I know," said Kara. "And guess what? Tomorrow's my big day. That's when we bust the body-snatching ring. I'll be back at Bingham in a few days."

"Good luck," Molly said. "And be careful."

"I will," said Kara. "Hey, Molly, remember how we used to wear our purple socks every Tuesday? Would you wear yours tomorrow, for good luck? I'll wear mine, too."

"Sure."

Kara felt a warm glow after her talk with Molly, but it didn't last long. That night, she had a terrible dream. Mr. Gino flooded the graveyard, and coffins floated to the surface with bodies spilling out. Kara was in a rowboat, trying to rescue corpses from Mr. Gino's grasp. Suddenly a skeleton rose from the swirling waters and spoke to her: "You! You must save us from that man."

Kara awoke in a cold sweat. The darkness in the room wanted to gobble her up. She reached for her Joan of Arc medal and held it tight.

After a while she felt better and padded downstairs to the family room. She sent Molly an e-mail alerting her to watch the evening news for a big surprise, then she packed up her supplies for the raid. Once her family woke up, Kara set off for school, saying she had to rehearse her speech.

"I'm really looking forward to your big day!" said her mom.

"Me too," said Kara. If she got out of this alive.

Chapter 25

STAKEOUT

A cold October wind had blown into town, bringing a misty fog with it. Pushed by the wind, Kara climbed the hill to St. Joan of Arc School.

Her breath formed white puffs in the air, and the wind whipped her hair. She ran the rest of the way to her toasty classroom.

Nicole was already there. "It's do or die. The ground's going to freeze tonight, and we can't dig for evidence after that."

"Don't worry. We're ready," Kara assured her.

Not much work got done, because everybody was in a frenzy about the afternoon celebration. At recess, kids poured onto the playground. They had a long recess so that the teachers could finish preparations. Kara huddled with her friends behind the Dumpster.

"First, I have to change my socks." Kara replaced her regulation blue socks with purple ones.

"What's that all about?" Nicole asked.

"It's an old tradition. Here, take these." Kara distributed walkie-talkies.

Breathing into the equipment, Nicole said, "Do you copy me?" The walkie-talkie crackled, then went dead.

"Oh, no! What are we going to do?" said Marisa.

"Never mind. We don't need this junk." Kara tossed the gear aside.

"You have the cell phone, right?" Marisa asked Nicole.

"No, my sister took it before I could."

Lines of worry creased Marisa's forehead. "But what if Mr. Gino's back there, and we need help?"

"I saw him before recess," Kara said. "He's inside, setting up for the event."

"Uh-oh," said Nicole. "Look behind you."

Kara turned to see Mr. Gino creeping along the edge of the cemetery. He was lugging a shovel, rake, and trash bag. The mist swallowed him up as he entered the woods.

"Good, we can catch him in the act," said Kara. "We'll take a few pictures, then run."

"Run for our lives, you mean," said Marisa, handing Nicole the camera. "I'm not going."

"Suit yourself." Nicole shoved the camera into her backpack and pulled out her map, accidentally ripping it. "Great! Now look what you've made me do."

Kara realized Nicole was scared. "Don't worry about the map. Marisa knows where the ditch is." Kara squeezed Marisa's cold hand. "Please, we need your help."

"I'm no chicken, but if we're going to do this, we need special protection." Marisa pulled a glass jar from her jacket.

"What's that?" Nicole asked.

"It's holy water, blessed by Father DiMarini." The girls bowed their heads as Marisa sprinkled water over them.

Kara clasped her medal and said, "St. Joan of Arc, mighty warrior, help us conquer the enemy. Guard us from evil and lead us to victory." She turned to her friends. "Let's go!"

The girls crept through the foggy cemetery and crawled into the woods. Marisa pointed to a stand of oak trees and said, "The ditch is that way."

Hunched over, the girls hobbled down a dirt trail. Kara listened for the sound of a shovel scraping the ground, but all she heard was the wind snapping branches and the chattering of squirrels. A big black bird swooped down and flew toward a clearing. Kara shivered. Vultures swarmed around dead bodies.

"Here, use these." Nicole passed Kara the binoculars. "I'll get the camera ready."

The woods were misty, but Kara was able to zoom in on the clearing. "There's Mr. Gino, over by a tree stump. Now he's picking up the bag, but I can't see what's in it."

She glanced at her friends and saw their eyes bugging out.

"I wonder whose body that is," said Nicole. "Did you notice our crossing guard is missing? I heard one of the teachers say he disappeared without a trace."

"Poor Mr. Mineo. We'll all end up in those graves," said Marisa.

Kara stared at her friends in disbelief. Marisa was shaking, and Nicole was gripping the camera so tightly her knuckles were white.

"Maybe we should wait," hedged Nicole. "We didn't get to rehearse like we planned."

"Only one person can stop Mr. Gino," said Marisa. "God."

So they were backing out! Well, Kara couldn't. Otherwise, she'd be on her way to the convent instead of back to Bingham.

"I'm going," she said, shoving things into her backpack. She sprinted along a path leading deep into the woods. As her feet pounded the earth, equipment jabbed her backbone. Gasping, she slowed to shift things around. A few moments later she heard footsteps behind her.

"Wait!" Nicole called. "I can't let you face that man alone."

"Me either," panted Marisa.

"This way, women!" Kara pushed past thorny bushes, kicked through brambles, and jumped over a creek. As she approached the clearing, she pressed a finger to her lips to warn her friends. The girls snuck behind a log and peeked out.

Down the trail, a stand of trees blocked her view, but Kara glimpsed something white through the branches. She took out her binoculars and spied three ghostly faces, shrouded in the mist.

"Nicole, look at this." Kara passed her the binoculars.

"How horrible! Three bodies hanging in trees!"

Marisa glanced through the binoculars. "It's out of focus, but I think those are statues. Why would he put them here?"

"Monuments to the dead," Kara said.

The girls crept closer. Mr. Gino was a few yards away, his back to them. He was working furiously, using a heavy rake to clear away leaves. The trash bag was beside him. Mr. Gino leaned his rake against a tree, then reached for his sack. Kara took out the camera and aimed it. Suddenly, she felt a sharp tap on her shoulder.

"Now what do we do?" a voice whispered.

Kara whirled around to see Anthony crouched behind her.

"What are you doing here?" she said, seething.

"I came to protect you guys. You think you can take on a six-foot man by yourself?"

"Get lost," hissed Nicole. Her fury seemed to energize her. She jumped up and called to Mr. Gino, "Show us the body in the bag!"

Mr. Gino looked up, his face a mix of astonishment and anger. "You can't come in here. It's not ready. Your time will come."

"No, your time has come!" said Kara. She vaulted toward him and tried to snatch the bag, but Mr. Gino had a tight grip. Nicole ran over, screaming like a banshee. With a howl of surprise, Mr. Gino dropped the sack. Marisa raced over, her black hair streaming behind her, and doused everyone with holy water.

"You kids get out of here or else!" threatened Mr. Gino.

"Or else what?" yelled Anthony. In all the commotion, he'd hidden behind a tree near Mr. Gino.

"Who's there?" Mr. Gino spun around, his feet landing on the metal prongs of his rake. The wooden pole smacked him in the forehead. Mr. Gino stumbled and sat down, groaning.

"Quick! While he's still out of it!" Kara said. She snapped a few pictures.

"Let's get out of here," Marisa said.

Anthony picked up one end of Mr. Gino's sack, and Kara and Nicole grabbed the other. Marisa ran ahead, leading the way back. Kara peered back once to see Mr. Gino still on the ground.

Nicole panted, "While Kara makes her speech, we'll dump the body onstage. That way everyone can see the truth for themselves."

Along the way, Kara told Anthony about the weird statues they'd seen.

"Probably zombies," Anthony said.

Huffing and puffing, the group reached the back door of the school auditorium.

"Uh-oh," Kara said. "We can't drag this onstage without Sister Mary Francis seeing us."

"I have an idea," said Anthony. "Kara and Marisa, you go first. Find Sister and distract her.

Then Nicole and I will sneak in and get the bag onstage. Maybe we can hide it behind the decorations."

"That's what I was going to say," Nicole sniffed.

Kara took a deep breath as she opened the auditorium door, hoping that Sister was not standing on the other side.

Chapter 26

BODY OF EVIDENCE

Luckily, Sister was nowhere in sight. In the back of the room, two TV crews were setting up, the seventh graders were practicing hymns, and Mrs. Shuey was fussing over a table of cake and punch. Kara looked up at the stage, which was draped with a red banner proclaiming the anniversary. A podium stood in the center, next to a row of chairs. Off to the side, Kara saw a big screen and a slide projector. Two huge floral bouquets topped a table covered in white cloth.

Marisa poked her. "There she is!"

Sister Mary Francis was across the room, almost hidden by enormous plants brought in to spruce up the place. She was talking to several important-looking people.

Kara opened the door, whispering, "Coast is clear." Anthony and Nicole slipped in as Marisa and Kara wove across the room toward the nun.

"Excuse me for interrupting, Sister," Kara said. "I had a question about my speech."

"Hello, girls," said Sister. "Archbishop Ryan, I'd like you to meet Kara McKinney and Marisa Yumzetti, two key leaders of the food drive."

The archbishop shook their hands. "God is smiling on your fine work."

Kara wondered if God would be smiling after her revelation about the bodies. She was pretty sure the archbishop wouldn't be.

Sister turned to a thin, balding man. "And this is Dr. Ludwig Klaus, a well-known scientist and former professor of mine."

Kara and Marisa exchanged glances. So a mad scientist had come to their event!

Last, Sister introduced a cheery woman with curly brown hair. "And this is Joanne Broadbent, head of the Harvest Food Bank."

"This is the most successful food drive any school has ever done!" Mrs. Broadbent said.

Out of the corner of her eye, Kara saw Anthony and Nicole dragging the bag across the stage.

Kara said, "Um, I wondered if you had a total for the food we collected, so I can mention it in my speech."

Mrs. Broadbent said, "Yes, we counted one hundred cases of food, which will fill three pickup trucks. That's just marvelous!"

Kara peeked at the stage. Anthony and Nicole were stuffing the bag under the table, which wobbled so much that a flower vase teetered close to the edge.

"The auditorium is filling up," remarked Sister. "We'd better be going."

Kara froze, unable to think of a stall tactic.

Marisa piped up, "Sister, do you have a minute to say hello to my grandmother and my parents? It would mean so much to them."

"Certainly," said Sister, and Marisa led her off.

When Kara glanced next at the platform, Anthony was sitting in a chair, the bag safely hidden. Nicole steadied the flower vase, wiped her forehead, and sat down.

Kara let out a long breath and crossed the room. Her parents waved, and she went over to say hello. To her surprise, Sister Blandina was with them.

"Kara dear, I need to talk to you about the retreat later today," Sister said.

For one crazy moment, Kara wanted to run from the nun. Her legs twitched, and a power pulsed from her purple socks. Then she calmed down, remembering that after today she wouldn't be going on any retreat.

Kara smiled at Sister Blandina and took her seat onstage. Sister Mary Francis was looking around anxiously.

Probably searching for Mr. Gino, Kara thought. She'd die if she knew the truth.

The music teacher struck piano chords as the seventh graders burst into song. Sister welcomed everyone and was followed by Father DiMarini, who heralded the school's tradition of education and community service.

Next, the mayor and archbishop droned on. Scanning the crowd, Kara spotted a policeman in the back, along with reporters holding tape recorders.

Kara whispered to Nicole, "Did you send out a press release?"

"Well, I did send out e-mail alerts this morning," Nicole said.

"Sh," Marisa murmured.

Finally, it was Kara's turn. Her walk across the stage seemed the longest of her life. She gripped the podium for support and said, "I want to thank everyone for contributing to our food drive. St. Joan of Arc students rallied together, because hunger is an issue that hits close to home. Last year the Harvest Food Bank served fifty thousand meals in our community. They do a wonderful job, and that's why we're donating a hundred cases of food that will fill three trucks!"

Everyone applauded. Kara saw her parents beaming.

"Our work can't stop today. On the table in the back, you'll find a fact sheet with locations of food banks, how to volunteer, and other information. Please get involved!" Kara urged.

"And now, Sister Mary Francis will reveal who won the contest for a day off from school." Kara stepped aside so that Sister could take the microphone.

Sister announced, "The winner is . . . the second grade class!"

The second graders went crazy, screaming and hooting.

"It was close," said Sister. "But Mr. Marty Boyd of Boyd Farms returned this weekend with thirty frozen turkeys, and those birds lifted the second grade to the top."

Suddenly, the back door of the auditorium swung open. In staggered Mr. Gino, a red welt on his forehead and his overalls covered in dirt. His dark eyes smoldered as he moved menacingly past the food table, past the TV crews, and up the aisles, approaching the stage.

Sister Mary Francis froze, and Kara grabbed the microphone. "I have another announcement to make. We must tell the truth about what's going on at this school."

Mr. Gino shouted, "Don't you dare reveal my secret!"

Sister hissed, "Kara, sit down!"

Kara plunged on: "Mr. Gino is digging up bodies in the graveyard, and he and Sister Mary Francis are conducting experiments on corpses. We have proof!"

Nicole and Anthony pulled out the bag, ripped it open, and dumped the contents across the stage. Hundreds of small gray objects rolled around.

"It's eyeballs! Shriveled-up eyeballs!" Nicole screamed.

The crowd gasped, and the TV reporters zoomed in for close-ups. The policeman buzzed toward the stage.

Anthony picked up a plastic container that had tumbled from the sack. "Worms! Body-eating worms."

Worried whispers rippled through the audience, and some kids jumped out of their seats. Kara saw Miss Monet sway, as if she were about to faint.

Father DiMarini took over. "Everyone, please calm down. Take your seats, and we will answer your questions. Mr. Gino, come to the podium."

Mr. Gino mounted the steps, glaring at Anthony and the girls, who scrambled back to their seats. Sister Mary Francis pulled the janitor aside, and they talked in hushed tones. Finally, Mr. Gino nodded and grabbed the microphone.

Chapter 27

AN UNEXPECTED ALIBI

"I am Gino Mastrantonio Zortea," he declared. "People here know me as Mr. Gino, the janitor, but I am also a landscaper and gardener. First, we will settle the matter of these mysterious objects."

He picked up some gray balls. "These are flower bulbs. The policeman can examine them. And these worms, they are good for the soil."

"Take them to the lab," called Nicole. The officer pocketed the samples.

Mr. Gino said, "And now for my announcement. I've built a garden, in honor of the school's anniversary. It's in the woods behind the cemetery."

Kara protested, "But we didn't see any garden, and we were just back there."

"You didn't quite make it to the garden,"

responded Mr. Gino. "Now I'll present a slide show of the work we've done."

The lights dimmed, and a picture popped up on the screen, showing the school's granite building and asphalt playground.

"Our school is wonderful, but it lacks green space," said Mr. Gino. "It's important for children and adults to have a garden, where they can meditate, pray, and enjoy nature. I brought this idea to Sister Mary Francis and Father DiMarini."

The next slide showed an area of charred wood and decaying plants. Mr. Gino said, "Father suggested this site, where the former church was located. It burned down years ago. I knew it would be challenging to grow a garden there, but I was willing to try."

Gino went on, "However, the only access was through the cemetery. I wanted to build a path, but the graveyard was too crowded."

Kara cried, "And that's when you began digging up bodies!"

"Yes, I did move bodies," Mr. Gino said.

The crowd murmured in disbelief.

Mr. Gino continued: "Father decided we should build a path from the rectory to the woods. But two graves were on the edge of the cemetery. I told Father I'd have to relocate them."

Anthony yelled, "And once you dug them up, you decided you could make money experimenting with corpses."

A vein in Mr. Gino's neck bulged. He's going to break down and confess, Kara thought.

"Not exactly," Mr. Gino said. "Father got permission from the descendants to relocate the graves, and he put the remains in a mausoleum."

"But we know you conducted experiments!" Nicole reached into her pocket and waved the e-mail.

"Yes, we did conduct experiments," Mr. Gino replied.

He flashed up a slide of a greenish tombstone, with the names Joseph and Maria Ricci. "To my amazement, this tombstone was covered with a rare ivy. I decided to transplant the ivy to my garden to see if it would thrive. Suddenly a new world opened up. Why not introduce other special plants, and make this garden something people would travel to see? I went to Sister Mary Francis, as we share an interest in botany."

Sister rose. "I majored in biology, with a minor in botany."

Mr. Gino continued: "Sister agreed to help, and Father said he'd pay the expenses. St. Joseph's University also provided a grant. You see, I attend night school at St. Joe's, where I'm getting a master's in landscape architecture."

"What a smoke screen!" said Nicole.

Mr. Gino ignored her. "My professors were very interested in one particular aspect of the project: restoring the statues I'd found."

"Your land-of-the-living-dead zombie statues," Anthony said.

Some people in the audience laughed.

Mr. Gino flashed another slide. Kara saw a marble statue of St. Joan of Arc, and others, too: Mary the Blessed Mother holding baby Jesus, and St. Francis of Assisi. They were all tangled in vines.

"These statues were part of the original church, but people forgot them after the fire," said Mr. Gino. "Restoring them was rewarding, but I also had hard labor to do. There were plants and trees on-site, but too many dead ones. I cleared them out and brought in new plants and trees, fertilizer, and mulch."

"Why didn't you tell everyone what you were doing?" Marisa asked.

"Sister and I wanted this to be a surprise for today's celebration. We also needed to be sure our experiments were working before we invited botanical experts here. I knew some students were curious, so I started working late at night to maintain secrecy."

"Save that story for the judge," mumbled Nicole.

"And now—the garden!" said Mr. Gino. The screen filled with a picture of a lovely terraced garden. The statues gleamed pearly white. Kara could almost hear the clanking of Joan of Arc's armor as the saint marched through the woods.

Sunlight pleated down through the trees, and formed pools of gold in an angel-sculpted fountain. Green wrought-iron benches had been placed near a brook, creating a sense of peace and solitude. Autumn flowers and bushes Kara had never seen before were in bloom.

Mr. Gino said, "I hope you'll enjoy this garden for years to come. Thank you."

Sister took over. "Thank you, Mr. Gino. We apologize for any confusion caused by our secrecy. I also want to give a hand to Kara and her committee for helping to present the new garden. We didn't want a boring slide show, so Kara and her friends provided the drama. Now please stay for refreshments and a garden tour."

Sister pulled Kara and her group aside, frowning. "Ask your parents to stay, so I can talk to them after the event." She lowered her voice and said, "You're history here."

Kara's heart lurched. It was one thing to get expelled herself, but another for her friends to get kicked out, too.

Chapter 28

CASE CLOSED

After the ceremony, Sister spoke with Kara's parents before being mobbed by the press. Sister bragged about the school's accomplishments and its garden. When a journalist asked about the body snatching, Sister smiled and said it was all part of the presentation.

"Can we talk to the kids?" asked a TV reporter.

"Kara McKinney is the spokeswoman, and her parents will allow her to be interviewed about the food drive only," said Sister.

Kara delivered snappy quotes while Marisa handed out fact sheets to reporters. Later, guests went off with Mr. Gino to tour the garden, while Sister Mary Francis huddled with Sister Blandina and

Miss Monet. After a while they beckoned the parents of Kara and her friends. A long discussion ensued.

"Oh, boy, are we in trouble," said Marisa as the gang hid in a corner.

At last, Sister Mary Francis called the kids over. Mr. Gino came, too, having finished the tour.

"I can't believe this situation got so out of hand," said Sister. "If you had suspicions or questions, you should have gone to your parents or a trusted adult."

The parents nodded vigorously.

"First, let's clear up any remaining questions," said Sister.

"Where did you bury the crossing guard?" Anthony demanded.

"Mr. Mineo?" Sister Mary Francis said. "He eloped in Jamaica, but he'll be back next week."

"Mr. Gino, your story doesn't hold up," Nicole said. "We found you digging in an area outside the garden."

"True," he replied. "I wanted to create a trail of flowers into the garden. I was rushing to plant the bulbs before the freeze, but I ran out of time."

Something else had been bothering Kara, since it was her first clue. "Do you eat candy when you work outside?"

"Guilty," said Mr. Gino. "But I've recently switched to sugarless gum."

Kara asked, "Who was the guy with the hearse?"

"My friend Rick. He drives a limousine, not a hearse, and he helped me install the benches and fountain."

Marisa said, "I don't have questions. I just want to forget about this."

"Well, you've made history today," stated Sister Mary Francis. "There's never been a presentation like this in the school's seventy-five years. We may have fooled the crowd, but you caused disruption, and you should do community service. Your parents agree, except for Kara's."

Kara stole a look at her parents, who were frowning.

"Kara, your parents will talk to you privately, but they agreed to let you hear out Sister Blandina, since she's shown so much interest in you."

Sister Blandina cleared her throat. "For your community service, you will spend six weekends at the Mother House doing charitable work. You also will attend the youth leadership retreat, so I can help you channel your energy and ideas appropriately."

Nicole and Anthony groaned. Only Marisa smiled.

Kara felt dazed. She didn't know what to think, and there wasn't time to sort it out. Her parents took her arm and sat her down in a chair in the back row.

"Kara, you're not doing community service," her father said.

"I'm not? Great!"

"We made a mistake enrolling you here," he continued. "We shouldn't have pulled you out of Bingham."

Her mother put her hands on her hips, "I enrolled you in Catholic school to give you a more structured, disciplined environment. But after what happened today, I see you've been running wild. You're going back to Bingham."

Kara couldn't believe it. At last, her parents were admitting they were wrong. She waited for joy to spread through every fiber of her being, for her arms to take wing and let her soar around the room.

Instead, she had a sinking feeling in her stomach. Suddenly Kara heard herself cry out, "But I want to stay here!"

"What?" said her mother. "You've done nothing but beg to go back to Bingham for the past month."

"But I have friends here. I've done all kinds of cool stuff. Bingham was really boring compared to this."

"You can't be learning much chasing after the janitor," said Mr. McKinney.

"That was an extracurricular activity!" Kara said. "My grades have been good. And how about the food drive—I learned about helping people."

Kara saw her mother's face soften, so she forged on. "And I'm learning how to be a better friend. Before, I only thought about what a friend should do for me."

"We'll talk this over tonight," said her father. "You can finish out the day here. We're going home."

Nicole, Marisa, and Anthony were standing by the stage, waiting for Kara.

"What happened?" Nicole asked.

"My parents want to pull me out of here," moaned Kara.

"Oh, no!" said Marisa, taking Kara's hand.

"But that's what you wanted." Nicole's shoulders drooped.

"I changed my mind," Kara said. "I really want to stay here. So what about you guys? Are you going to the Mother House?"

Nicole sighed. "Yeah, our parents copped a plea bargain for us."

Anthony whispered, "Wait till you hear this. My great-aunt lives at the Mother House, and there's strange stuff going down there. Some of the nuns' wheelchairs have been stolen. And the Sisters are being forced to work long hours. I also hear that they're harboring a fugitive."

"It sounds like they need our help!" said Nicole. "But it won't be fun without you, Kara. How can we get your parents to change their minds?"

"I'll ask Sister Blandina and Miss Monet to call them, and I'll promise to do double chores at home," Kara said. "But I need more ideas, or I'm history here."

"We'll help you," said Marisa, and they all bent their heads to come up with a plan.